Stumptown

S.W. Campbell

Published by Shawn Campbell

Stumptown

Stumptown

ISBN: 978-1-7332314-4-2

To Grammie,
You were the best grandmother a kid could ask for.
I miss you every day.

Stumptown

Table of Contents

Preface

I originally conceived of the idea of *Stumptown* in 2013 as a series of interconnected stories revolving around the lives of a group of friends and associates in their late twenties to early thirties living in Portland, Oregon. Given that at the time I had just turned 30, it wasn't that hard of a concept to imagine Looking back now, the world of 2013 seems almost foreign given all that has happened since, with much of what seemed so important at the time merely a symptom of much of the chaos that has since followed. However, when this project was first conceived, it seemed an important moment in time to try and capture. It's difficult to describe. Though the Great Recession had involved repeated punches to the gut, the golden promise of opportunities for a better world still seemed intact, at least from a distance. It wasn't until one bothered to look closer that the growing cracks began to appear. If the feeling of the time could be summed up, I would say hopeful yet unsure. Enough memories of the world in which we had once lived still existed to keep us from realizing we were living in a new world all together.

Portland was of course the perfect setting for such a collection of stories, especially as it was viewed in the early and mid-2010's. To many people, Portland was seen as some kind of quirky utopia, where the social sins of the past could be laid to rest and we could all go forward arm in arm together into the brightening sunshine. Many people, unencumbered by the deeply driven roots of age, flocked to Portland in pursuit of this dream. Of course, as the pilgrims were eventually forced to learn, this was all complete bullshit. Problems exist everywhere and are not something from which you simply walk away.

The characters of *Stumptown* were never meant to address such broad ideas. They were meant to be just normal everyday people, living their lives as best they could, navigating their day to day, with hints of the broader sense of the world viewable only by the reader. The first character to appear was Paul, a man of simple needs, battering his way through the world. At the time, I must have felt that the name Paul was the perfect example of an everyman, since it was also the name of the main character in my first novel, *The Uncanny Valley*, though they were never meant to be the same person. Paul began with a story told to me by a friend at a campout, though Paul was never meant to represent my friend. Rather, he was an amalgamation of many different people, his appearance largely left undescribed, with him identifiable more by his general demeanor. In total, Paul has appeared as a main character in around ten of my stories, plus as a side character in numerous more. However, only half of them have ended up in this book, with the rest focused on other times in his life.

Originally, Paul was meant to be the only main character in *Stumptown*. However, writing just about him soon grew tiresome. While not a bad character, he had developed into a rather plodding human being, stubbornly accepting the world in which he found himself. Due to this, other characters began to thrust themselves forward as the main focus of stories. The first of these was Devin, a woman quietly asserting herself in the world, and then came the more chaotic Leo, and then several others. Similar to Paul, many of the stories for these characters were based on tales I heard from friends, though the characters themselves were amalgamations of many people. In many ways these stories were putting into practice one of the oldest of writing exercises. I was basically taking the characters I had developed and putting them into the situations described to me to see how they would react. However, it would be a lie to say that the situations themselves did not lead to the characters developing in ways that I had not originally planned. Such is the writing process.

At one point, my idea for *Stumptown* became having several stories for each character, but unfortunately this idea fell to the wayside. I never worked specifically just on the Stumptown stories, as I called them in my head, and eventually the never ending progression of time caught up with me. By the time 2017 rolled around, the world had changed, and my enthusiasm for the project was waning. As a short story collection, *Stumptown* was meant to explore the uncertainties tucked quietly away. It was hard to see the point of building it out further once we shifted from dealing with them by pretending they didn't exist to shouting at each other about them as loudly as possible.

I spent the remainder of 2017 writing a few last stories about Paul and his friends specifically designed to push the collection's overarching narrative to the foreground. The last story about Paul was written in 2018. Not having enough of such material on its own, I then played around with ideas of how to get the collection up to my expectations concerning length without disturbing the theme. For a time I considered adding in the stories about other parts of Paul's life, but in the end did not include them given that I felt they would distract rather than support the overall point of the collection. Instead, I chose to include other stories I had written, all circling around the same idea and set in the same location. The completion of *Stumptown* was then further delayed by my first short story collection, *An Unsated Thirst,* and then by my second novel, *Papaya*. However, I'm glad to say that it is now complete.

I hope nothing that I have written in this preface takes away from the reader's enjoyment of these stories. Though published in a different world then what I had originally envisioned, I still believe them to be relevant and worth the read. Though individually they don't touch on big ideas, I believe collectively they hold a certain truth about us. I don't think we can fully understand where we are now without trying to understand where we were then. I hope you enjoy the read.

Glimpses of Morning

The Max train slows as it approaches before sliding to a halt. The doors open and my fellow commuters, my surrogate family, and I shuffle in like cattle being loaded onto trailers to start our journey to slaughter. The train is full. Passengers from earlier stops already fill the seats. The majority of us newbies are forced to stand. Most of us are not old enough or pregnant enough to warrant an act of chivalry. I bend my knees and lean my body forward as the Max jerks into motion. I feel pride at my skill at remaining upright without gripping the polished bar or plastic hand loops. In my head I imagine another passenger noticing my skill and thinking, 'wow look at that guy standing up on the train without support. He must be a badass.' These are but the musings of boredom. My skills go unnoticed.

Every morning it's the same thing. The alarm goes off and I force myself from the warm embrace of blankets and sheets piled haphazardly, loose and not tucked in. The alarm is set away from the bed, forcing me to get out of my haven. If I set the alarm within arm's reach there is the chance that I will shut it off in my sleep. Up out of bed. Turn off the alarm. Fingers on a chalkboard for my psyche. Take a shower. Remind myself to buy more shampoo. Wonder why the shampoo always runs out faster than the conditioner. Eat breakfast. This week it's Captain Crunch with Crunch Berries. Get dressed in clothes that I don't want to wear. Double check to make sure I have everything I need in my briefcase. Walk to the Sunset Transit Center and wait for the Max.

It's a strange thing to get sucked into a routine. To start feeling like every day is the same as the last. There are minor differences. There are always minor differences, but in essence everything stays the same. I stand on the platform, today glad it's not raining, surrounded by people I recognize but do not know. The people who join me are the same people every day. They are more familiar to me than the majority of my family and friends. I see them more consistently.

There's Business Lady Who Wears Too Much Lipstick, Fella Who Works Out A Lot, Pink Haired Girl, Shaved Head Dude, Attractive Professional Who Wears Low Cut Blouses, Woman I'd Like to Kiss, and Balding Guy In Suit. Constant companions I know nothing about. If any are missing it's instantly noticeable. Where is About Time To Retire Man? Is he sick today? Maybe he caught an earlier train, or was a little late and missed this one. His absence is noted and forgotten.

Over a hundred different universes are packed into the train around me. People so close you could reach out and physically touch them. So close but still millions of miles away. All follow the unwritten rules of the Max. Avoid eye contact. If you make eye contact look away as quickly as possible. No talking to anyone else. Talking is only allowed if you know somebody from outside the Max or if something happens that affects the whole group. Avoid acknowledging the existence of others as much as possible.

Many people on the Max have built up their walls as high as they will go. They send texts, read books, or wear earbuds, listening to music or podcasts. I do none of these things. To me these tools seem like crutches for the unwell. People who cannot stand to be alone. Some people have to constantly distract themselves. Fill their heads with outside stimuli to avoid their own disturbing thoughts. Hiding from self-conscious doubts and realizations of their own failings. Others need the noise because their heads are empty, containing nothing of interest to themselves or others.

I don't know why I judge people like this. Why I think of myself as their better? It's a point of pride for something that only exists in my mind. Perhaps it's that inherit want to feel special and unique. The need to feel like I'm somehow a cut above the rest of the herd. I'm not special. I'm no better. There's no way to know what's happening in others' heads. I have the same failings as the rest of humanity. I'm just another one of the sheep.

I stand and stare out at the streets and roads flashing past. Watching the cars moving alongside us on the freeway, competing in an imaginary race of which they know nothing about. The outside world grows boring. My attention shifts. Route maps line the wall. Today I'll memorize all the stations on the Red Line in order from west to east. Perhaps tomorrow I'll do the Yellow Line. Safety posters are plastered above the windows. Don't eat on the Max. No pets except for service animals. No loud talking on your phone. Give up your seat to the disabled and elderly.

The poster for giving up your seat has people getting up for an unseen person. Judging by the looks on their faces the person must be terribly disfigured. The poster asking you to not have loud phone conversations has a Hispanic woman in the throes of an intense conversation, oblivious to those around her. An obviously perturbed Samuel L. Jackson doppelganger looks on.

Congratulations to Annette Benning, Tri-Met employee of the year. I wonder what she did to earn that honor. Maybe her bus was always on time. At the very least she probably didn't hit anybody with it.

We glide into the big tunnel. I glance away from the signs and start looking at the people around me. If everybody is avoiding noticing everybody else, then somebody like me can watch everybody without them noticing. People are much more interesting to watch than the same old scenery and the same old posters. My eyes search the faces, all neutral and bored, and look for those who have let their guard down. Here we all are, standing or sitting in a steel box surrounded by people, and yet we can forget all of it. People work so hard to ignore those around them that they forget that they are there themselves. They forget that they're not alone, and for just a moment, let their guard down. Emotions flash across their faces.

None of us can read minds, but we can all read emotions. We can all empathize. For just a moment I can feel a connection with a total stranger. An understanding that though all of our universes are different, they all exist based upon the same rules. Our thoughts and memories are what make us independent and unique. Our emotions are the physics that tie us all together and make us all the same. In the end we all want the same thing. Somebody to connect with, somebody to care, somebody who will not turn away. More smiles than tears, more elation than despair, more victories than defeats. For just a moment I can let my own guard down and know I'm not alone. For a moment I can pretend that I've found what I've been looking for and that nothing is missing.

It's only just for a moment. People can feel when they're being watched. A tickling in their subconscious. They turn and look me in the eye and all the defenses pop back into place, both theirs and mine. They know what I've seen. Sometimes they look quickly away, avoiding prolonged eye contact, embarrassed that they've let their guard down. Sometimes they give me a look of disgust as though I'm a voyeur, like I've forced my way into their house and rummaged through things.

Sometimes they try to stare back until I look away, to reassert their dominance over their lives by asserting their dominance over the one who saw their weakness. The first one to look away is the one who is the most afraid. It's a battle of the wills, a battle that I can't let myself lose. I'll not roll over on my back and show my belly. We stare at each other, sometimes for as long as a minute, keeping our faces neutral, hiding our discomfort. It's rare that I don't win in these contests.

Sometimes, but more rarely, they look up and make no attempt to hide their emotions. They look back at me unafraid and it all pours out of them. For some they are at peace. They don't mind that others can see what they have within. For others their minds are chaos and breaking down. Their emotions have become a flood which their bodies can no longer contain. My greatest hope and my worst fear. When these people look up I'm always the first to avert my gaze.

The moment is gone and I'm alone again. The connection is broken. I shake my head and look back out the window, staring outward at the darkness of the tunnel flashing past. I'm not the only one to do this. I'm not the only one who searches the sea of faces. The roles have been reversed at times. I've felt other's eyes on me. I've felt my own defenses penetrated. The response I have often differs. It's based entirely upon how I feel at the time. Sometimes I look away. Sometimes I stare back in defiance. Sometimes I stare back and don't care what they see. When I stare back in defiance I take pride in making them look away, in making them feel like they've done something wrong.

While searching the sea of faces I at times catch the eye of someone who is doing the same. For a moment we just stare at one another. A mutual understanding. The sight of a kindred spirit. The moment passes and we both look away. We both know that we can't get what we're looking for from the other, so we both move on. We want to explore other universes, but not let others explore ours. Neither of us is willing to take the risk, and so, the one thing we really want lies just out of reach.

The Max emerges from the dark tunnel and begins its constant stop and start through downtown. My surrogate family begins to drift away, exiting as they reach their stops. Pink Haired Girl gets off at Goose Hollow. Fella Who Works Out A Lot exits at PGE Park. The train jerks to a halt at the Library, my stop. I push through the mass of people to the door and get out as I always do. Balding Guy In Suit also gets off. He begins to walk east, towards the rising sun which is still hidden behind the tall buildings of downtown. I round the corner and head north up Tenth Avenue towards my office.

The walk from the Max station to my office is twenty blocks if I walk the quickest course. My route normally adds an additional two blocks so I can walk by the yoga studio with the big window. The air is crisp and clean. The streets are slightly damp from a rain earlier in the morning. Few people are on the street at this hour. A smattering of business people walking to work, garbage men and street cleaners going through their morning routine, and homeless people roused by the police and told to move along. Things are quiet.

The movement of everybody changes the dynamic. On the Max we're all companions of circumstance. Forced to spend a large amount of time together in a tightly packed enclosed space. On the streets we're more free. There's more chaos on the streets. You rarely see the same person twice. People move in a constant ebb and flow. There's no chance to study the people around you. Connections are quick and fleeting. If they're walking in the opposite direction then you only catch a glimpse. Maybe they look away and avoid eye contact. Maybe they stare, their faces neutral. Maybe you get lucky and they look you full in the face and smile. Most of the time I smile back. At least when I feel up to it.

If people are walking in the same direction you never see their faces. There's nothing to study but their backsides, which can be nice at times, but is no good for feeling a connection with the world around you. Today I find myself walking behind a group of people. After a few blocks the majority peel off one direction or another, leaving just me and an attractive blonde woman. I speed up and walk past her so she doesn't feel uncomfortable. I don't want her to feel apprehensive about the strange solemn man walking behind her.

At the end of each block I stop, look both ways, and then cross if there are no cars coming. I ignore the walk and don't walk signs. What is the point of waiting if there are no cars coming? I've done this walk several hundred times. I could do it with my eyes closed if I needed to. All is in its place. All is right where it's supposed to be. There are changes, but they're so minute and happen so slowly that I don't notice them.

My coat is not thick enough to keep out the chill. I wore my lighter coat today. It's getting to be the time of year when it's very cold in the morning, but warm throughout the day and evening. I turn into the usual coffee shop and order a hot chocolate. I hope that one of the blonde baristas is working today. I'm disappointed. Today I'm served by the old woman who likes to wear tight shirts and doesn't believe in wearing a bra. I try not to stare at the hanging pendulums that all the world can see, but it's hard to look away, even when you find something unpleasant and it makes you uncomfortable. I guess it's more my hang up than hers.

My hot chocolate in hand I continue my journey towards my office. Small black birds sing to each other in the trees. I step around a pile of what I hope is dog shit. People walk past me going about their business. I'm surrounded by people but still feel like the only person on the planet. It's a strange feeling.

Here is the place where I was accosted by the bum last month. He had walked up and for no good reason began yelling obscenities at me. I had ignored him and walked on. A pretty brunette had walked up to me and commented how weird it was. I agreed and kept walking. I often wonder what would've happened if I had struck up a conversation with her.

There's no use dwelling on such things. The opportunities have passed and you can only move forward. Never back. I look up at the windows in the buildings above me. I don't know what I expect to see. Maybe I'll see a murder, or two people having sex, or just someone walking around with their bathrobe open, eating crackers. The chances are low, but I always feel compelled to look. If I fail to do so I might miss something new and exciting. Something I haven't seen before.

I feel like I'm in a rut. One day bleeds into another. One week becomes the next. Only the changing of the weather marks the passage of the months. I need to make a change. I need to do something before I go insane. I take a right and then a left and proceed to walk up Ninth Avenue instead of Tenth. I crane my head and marvel at the strange buildings around me. I'm only one block from my usual route, but it's as though I'm in a whole different city.

A woman walks up the street towards me. Her hair is black and curly. She's of an average height with a hourglass shape. Leather boots, tight jeans, turtleneck sweater, leather coat, scarf, and a cabby hat. She's attractive. She has one of those walks where her hips rise up and down like the gentle rocking of a boat. It's a nice thing to walk past. She's talking on her phone. I only catch a snatch of the conversation before she moves past. Her voice is shrill with shock, disgust, and exasperation.

"I don't care if he's your best friend! I don't want to gang bang!"

I hold it together until she rounds the corner and turns out of sight. Painfully stifled giggles erupt from me in great guffaws which echo through the empty streets. An out rushing of hilarity at the ridiculousness of the situation which I had just walked by. What the hell did the guy's best friend do for him? The only scenario that makes sense in my mind involves heroically saving his life in the war. I shake my head and keep walking, smirking and chuckling to myself. Feeling lucky that I've never found myself facing issues such as the ones contained in the universe which rolled past on the phone.

I walk past the yoga studio where the women and one man, either very confident or very pervy, do stretches for all to see, yet still give you dirty looks if they catch you looking. I watch them from the corner of my eye as I walk past. I reach my office and get in the elevator. I ride the elevator to the top floor and get out. I unlock my office door, walk in, and sit down. As my computer slowly loads the thought of the woman on the cellphone bubbles up in my mind and I chuckle to myself again, at least until a new realization crosses my mind. I'm but an observer. I've had many friends, but I've never had one I would describe as that good of a friend.

Stumptown

Slap Fight

"Fuck you!"

The sharp exclamation echoed across the block, breaking Paul's train of thought as he lay in his bed, staring upward at the shadows amongst the high ceiling, suffering another sleepless night. The voice hit him like a hammer. In an instant all of his thoughts were scattered and his mind was led astray. All the conversations that existed only his head, all the clever quips and logical rhetoric, all the images of Lisa nodding finally in understanding. The imagined end of all the problems between the two of them, all the fights and all the hurts. All disappeared with the shout. He glanced at the alarm clock. It's red digital face showed 2:33 AM.

Curiosity killed the cat, but it had nothing on Paul. He pulled aside the blankets and swung his feet onto the cold hardwood floor. Up went the blinds, flooding the small shabby bedroom with the diffuse light of a nearby street lamp. Squinting against the sudden change in ambiance, Paul slid open the window, the old wood frame grating as it rose, and leaned out to look at the sidewalk below.

Paul stuck his head out just in time to see the silvery flash of a fixed gear bicycle fly through the air, striking a man in the face. The man's fedora flew off his head into the gutter as he fell back onto the sidewalk. Blood began to pour from his nose. His upturned moustache was so heavily shaped with wax that the blood flowed around it and down onto his chin. Small droplets dribbled down, satin stains on his blue flannel shirt.

His assailant was a mirror image except for his flannel shirt being brown and the addition of a bushy beard and turtle shell glasses. The assailant gave another scream, this one more animal sounds than words, and charged forward. Blue Shirt on the ground raised up a leg in skin tight jeans and connected a leather shoe into the brown shirted man's gut. Brown Shirt reeled backward with a grunt, giving Blue Shirt man time to rise and wipe his nose with his sleeve, a thick streak of red across the blue.

Brown Shirt rushed at him again and the two connected in battle. Open limp wristed hands flew back and forth in a flurry nearly too fast to follow. Occasionally the dry slap of palm on skin could be heard as one or the other landed a blow. Sometimes one would attempt to push the other away, and the two would separate and circle for a moment like angry dogs, before rushing back into grapple and pummel each other once again. Neither seemed able to gain the upper hand, neither would commit enough to cause much damage to the other. Both appeared afraid of leaving an opening that might cause them undue pain and discomfort if it was exploited.

After a minute of such dancing the two separated. The brown and the blue stood warily facing each other. Both were slightly stooped, their chests rising and falling as they sucked in precious oxygen. The eyes of Blue Shirt were cold and angry. The eyes of Brown Shirt were watery and near overflowing. Blue Shirt stabbed forward a harsh accusatory finger.

"You threw your god damn bike at me! What the hell man!"

"How could you do it? How could you not invite me? For god sakes, I was the one who introduced the two of you! I've been friends with both of you for as long as I can remember!"

"You know why you can't come. You know the fucking reason. You need to let it go."

"You didn't even want to talk to her at that party. You were too scared. I had to bring her over and do most of the talking. She wouldn't have even given you the time of day if it wasn't for me."

"Just leave it alone."

"No, I won't leave it alone. This is horseshit. I only did what the two of you asked me to do, and now I'm getting completely kicked out of your lives."

"Look, it was a mistake. It changed things. It was either quit hanging out with you or lose her. I love her. I'm sorry, but that's just the way it is."

"I deserve to be at your wedding."

"Deserve?! It's my god damn wedding. You don't tell me you deserve to go to my god damn wedding. You're just mad because both of us picked each other instead of you. You can't even be happy for us. It all has to be about you."

"It's like you don't even understand."

"No, I understand, I just don't fucking care."

"You bastard. I'll fucking kill you!"

Brown Shirt's face contorted until it could barely even be called human. He took a step forward and his arm moved quick as a snake. Blue Shirt's head whipped back as the slap caught him across the cheek with a loud crack, dropping him to one knee. He stayed there. Brown Shirt stood above him, a triumphant lion over his kill, tears flowing down his face, and his voice choked with snot and emotion.

"You two asked me to do it. I did it because I care about
both of you. I'm not ashamed of what we did. Is that what it is?
Are you ashamed of what happened? Are you afraid that people
will see me and make comments behind their hands? Is that it?
Maybe you're afraid that just you isn't going to be enough
anymore. Are you scared that maybe she wants to do it again?"

Blue Shirt looked up. His eyes narrowed. He had blood on
his face and a perfect red hand mark on his cheek.

"Shut your face. You're not coming to my fucking
wedding."

"Fuck your wedding, maybe I'll come to your honeymoon. I
bet she'd like that."

Everything on Blue Shirt straightened at the same time.
Knees, back, arm; all rose up as one. The fist connected solidly
under the bearded chin, lifting Brown Shirt off of us his feet.
His legs went out from under him and he collapsed into a pile on
the sidewalk, a lump boneless flesh. Blue Shirt stepped over him
and picked up his fedora, placing it on his head. He turned back
to look at his fallen opponent and spit in his general direction.

"Stay the fuck away from us."

Blue Shirt turned and walked down the street, disappearing
around the corner. Brown Shirt lay on the ground, sobbing like a
child, his body convulsing. The trembling form sat in the exact
center of the light cast by the overhead street lamp, like an actor
in a play, waiting for the curtains to come down and for the show
to be at an end.

Paul leaned back and shut the window, wood scraping
against wood. He pulled down the blinds and the room returned
to darkness. Paul fumbled back to his bed, his eyes not yet
adjusted, climbed back in, and pulled the covers over his legs
and chest. Paul sat in the dark and waited for the barrage of
thoughts to come for him again. The maddening cycle that
fueled his sleepless anxiety. The tears for happy memories. The
pleading for her to stay. The wishes that the world of old would

return again. The anger. The worrying. The sadness. They did not come. There was just a skinny hipster in a brown flannel shirt crying on the sidewalk, mourning a world that would never be again. Paul closed his eyes and drifted off into the warm embrace of dreamless sleep.

Lost Dog

The poster says *Lost Dog*. At first I think it's a poster for a lost cat. There are always a lot of those around. Posters plastered with feline photos of strangely named house cats and paragraphs of adoration filled with terms that most people avoid using even when talking of their progeny or their spouse. Posters put up by people who refuse to accept the natural order of the world and the fact that their catnip addicted friend has most likely been eaten by coyotes which are the natural by-product of the demand for sprawling wilderness green space in the middle of the urban jungle.

Part of me when I see such signs, the part that wants to do bad things which are neither empathetic or within the standards of polite societal decorum, wants to call the number written before me and let them know in no uncertain terms that their cat is surely dead and it would most likely be better for all involved if they just moved on. But I don't. It's not so much because I worry what the world will think of me for such digressions. No, it's more along the lines that I can remember several once living

favorite mini-lynx's now just memories of a childhood which is
my own.

Of course the coyote assumption isn't really fair. Not every
cat that goes missing has fallen victim to the short end of the
food chain. Memories float back to friends of a certain ex who
once had their kitty catnapped by a probably more than slightly
unbalanced neighbor. The lovely couple would let their cat, I
think his name was Boris, out to frolic in the night, unleashing a
terror in the darkness on the neighborhood's unwitting rodents,
birds, and squirrels. The nosey neighbor next door likened these
nightly releases as equal to cat abuse and Boris soon found
himself tricked inside for a tasty morsel and was never seen
again. It was really amazing to see how little power the police
have in such matters of tabby ownership.

I don't have long to stay. I still have a ways left in my run
and if I stand around too much in the cold December air my
sweat will start to freeze and my joints will start to stiffen.
Much like an old car I'll find it difficult to get my motor to
turnover. But this poster, for a dog named Judy, catches my eye,
and I stop to stare for a bit at the little black furry face framed by
a doggy moustache and a tiny tuft gray beard. There's really
nothing special about this poster or this dog, except of course the
fact that I saw Judy running happily along when I topped out on
Terwilliger just half an hour ago.

Now some may think it unfair that I so cheerfully doom the
kitties to their grave while planning a one man search for a
doggy gone astray. But you must understand that my childhood
was filled with more favorite dogs than beloved cats. It's not
that one is better than the other. It's just that in my memories the
dogs had a greater amount of permanence than the cats. Plus, I
like dogs more, there's no denying that.

Before you start thinking too well of me, your head filled
with images of me marching off on a heroic quest to return the
poor lost canine to her owners, you should probably know that I

don't have any intention of searching for the dog. It's not that I am cold hearted, uncaring, or a just plain lazy. Though I have been a little bit of all three from time to time. But reading the sign before me again and again does little to spur me into action.

Lost Dog

Judy was last seen on December 16 on Highway 99W near I-5 in the Fantasy Video parking lot. She went missing when Grandma fell carrying her down a flight of stairs. If you see her please call immediately.

My head is full of questions for which I don't really want any answers. I continue on my run without taking note of the contact number. Maybe some will think me crass. Maybe some will think me a bit of a heartless jerk. But there are certain circumstances I just don't want to be in any way directly involved in, even if I am really curious to know more about the story. Besides, given the details from the poster, there's a good chance that maybe Judy is happier outside.

Margarita Monday

The beeping of the EKG machine is an annoyance. Each beat of the living corpse's heart is like a finger poking Paul right behind the eyes. It isn't a sharp and painful feeling, nor is it a constant dull ache. It's more like pressing one's hand against a recent bruise. Pressure, then no pressure, pressure, then no pressure. Paul blinks his eyes and tries to ignore the sensation. It could be a lot worse. Relatively speaking this is only a slight annoyance.

"Scalpel."

The voice is harsh and filled with irritation. Paul looks up from the EKG into the fuming brown eyes of Dr. Stone across the table. Dr. Stone's brown eyes radiate anger, but then again, they always seem to radiate anger. Even with the majority of his face covered by his surgical mask, his eyes are enough to express his displeasure with the world around him. This is the second time that Dr. Stone has asked for the scalpel. Paul failed to hear him the first time.

Paul looks at the others clustered around the table. Across from him Dr. Philip's green eyes are filled with worry, concern that Paul will soon incur the wrath of Dr. Stone. Next to Dr. Stone, Lisa's blue eyes give Paul a dirty look. A co-conspirator eyeing the probable weakest link in their shared secret. When she notices Paul noticing her back, her eyes shift to asking Paul what right he has to look at her. Dr. Cohen, the anesthesiologist, leans against the wall, his eyes half closed, looking bored.

Paul shakes his head to clear it. He needs to have a clear mind. He has to get his head into the game. He picks up the sharpened instrument and hands it to Dr. Stone, miming his incantation as he does.

"Scalpel."

Paul doesn't want to make Dr. Stone mad. Dr. Stone's anger is legendary amongst the other staff members of the hospital. The staff pass around folk tales of Dr. Stone, most second hand, which seem larger than life and far to the implausible side of the reality scale. Dr. Stone destroyed the career of a young orderly that once accidentally took his parking space. Dr. Stone threw a phone across the lobby when a chatty receptionist failed to get the chart he wanted fast enough. Lisa had told him the other day that she had heard that Dr. Stone once threw his surgical instruments at a newly hired nurse in the middle of an appendectomy after the nurse had failed to meet his exacting standards. The nurse had been so traumatized that he quit the next day. Paul is in a condition where he needs to be more careful.

The first margarita had made Paul feel relaxed. It had been a long day at the hospital and he had felt like he needed to unwind. The second margarita had made him feel good. It had pushed away the problems to another day. The third margarita had changed him internally. His bones, once all stiff and rigid, had softened and become rubbery, pliable in unexpected directions. The fourth margarita had removed all of his bones, allowing him to bend in ways he was not supposed to bend. The fifth margarita had converted him from a solid into a liquid. They had poured him into the taxi which he and the other nurses had taken home.

The vomiting the night before had helped. Paul would've definitely been unable to be here today if he had not puked. When he had first woken up he had felt a little woozy, but some tomato juice and bread had soon solved that problem. Even with all the preventatives he hadn't escaped unscathed. It is only slightly distracting, not debilitating. Lisa seems unaffected by the night before. She's as alert and quick as ever. This is all well and good. Lisa is doing all the grunt work today, assisting the doctors with suction and the other messier ends of the surgery. Paul only has to watch the living corpse's vitals, hand over tools when asked, and keep count of everything to make sure nothing gets left inside.

"Making the incision."

Dr. Stone's voice is monotone, a sharp cut across the cold air of the surgery center. Paul can feel the words slice across the distance between them, enter his ears, and flick his bruised brain. Again, not painful, just annoying. Paul watches Dr. Stone as he works. Dr. Stone is an asshole, all surgeons are assholes, but he is also a good surgeon. It is a simple laparotomy, a large single cut across the abdomen, a cut Dr. Stone has done a hundred times before.

Paul feels his nose itch and wishes he could scratch it. But of course he cannot. This is a clean room and his face is encased in his surgical mask and his hands are encased in rubber gloves. Paul feels sweat begin to form on his brow. Cool air blows from vents above, but it does not matter. His body feels hot. It is working hard to remove the last lingering toxins. A bead of liquid coldness moves from between his shoulder blades down his spine. He can imagine the stale smell of tequila wafting from his pores.

The scalpel lifts, pulls back, and drops again. The initial cut is deepened, revealing the white of the lineus alba underneath. Another lift, another shift, and another cut. They are through another layer of tissue. Paul looks at the vitals again. All seem to still be normal and stable. The chest of the living corpse rises and falls with every breath.

The living corpse is not dead, but in a way it is easier to deal with surgeries if Paul imagines that it is. A living corpse has all the same vitals and automatic responses as a living person, but none of the thoughts, dreams, and history. Watching someone work on a living corpse is like watching someone working on a car. It is easier if it is just a machine going under the knife, not a living person. If one thinks too much about the living corpse they are working on, if they begin to feel empathy for the person encased in the organic vehicle, things could become overwhelming.

"Hemostats."

Paul hands the hemostats to Dr. Philips and Dr. Stone.

"Hemostats."

They look like giant tweezers. Lisa suctions blood away from the incision. The hemostats lift part of the revealed peritoneum, the lining of the abdominal cavity. Dr. Stone cuts a hole where the hemostats hold the tissue tight, exposing the bodily innards to the outside world. The smell of the living corpse's body cavity enters the cool air of the room, like a raw steak at room temperature. Paul feels bubbles in his own gut shift, creating an uncomfortable pressure that wasn't there before. This has nothing to do with the surgery. He has aided in many before and it has never bothered him. This is an internal problem.

The first margarita had made Paul content to sit and watch his fellow nurses try their hand at karaoke. The second margarita had convinced him to stand up and give it a go with his own rendition of *Sweet Caroline*. The third margarita had

given him the courage to ask Lisa to dance. The fourth
margarita had consoled him when she had said no. The fifth
margarita had given him the fortitude to dance by himself,
despite the fact that his dancing shared more aspects with a
seizure than rhythmic movements.

"Scissors."

Paul takes the scalpel from Dr. Stone and hands him the
scissors.

"Scissors."

Dr. Stone inserts his fingers into the freshly cut hole in the
peritoneum and lifts it away from the intestines inside. The
scissors work along the tissue, enlarging the initial hole and
revealing the guts underneath. Paul can never look at a person's
digestive system without thinking of his old college girlfriend.
Her grandmother had been off the boat Chinese and had still
made many traditional Chinese dishes with pig offal, which she
got at the local butcher. Paul would sometimes go over to her
house, and see the old woman cleaning them in the sink.
Stretching the intestines and kneading them with her fingers.

Paul's gut gurgles once again. A bubble shifts higher in his
own intestines, displaced as heavier gases work their way down
his internal tubes. The beeping of the EKG and the whir of the
fans covers the noises of his digestive issues. Nobody else
notices. Nobody else hears. Paul tries to ignore the bubbling.
He concentrates on the living corpse's gastrointestinal issues,
ignoring his own.

The movements of Dr. Stone and Dr. Philips are not much
different than the work of the old Chinese woman. Their hands
run along the pink tube of the small intestine, looking and
searching for the obstruction. The living corpse had come in a
week ago, complaining of abdominal pain and swelling. The
corpse had been in for a minor surgery, to correct a perforated
peptic ulcer, a few months before. An x-ray had shown an
obstruction in the small intestine. Initial attempts to clear the

29

obstruction, enemas and nasogastric tubes, had failed to make things better. Surgery had become the best option.

The first margarita had been accompanied just by peanuts from a bowl on the bar. Peanuts undoubtedly infected by germs of every other patron who had touched them. The second margarita had been accompanied by his share of a helping of nachos, heavy on the jalapenos and queso. The third margarita had been accompanied by a spicy burrito, the specialty of the house. The fourth margarita had been accompanied by more than his share of a second helping of nachos, even heavier on the queso and jalapenos. The fifth margarita had been accompanied by nothing except an extra lime which he had stolen from the tray on the bar when the bartender wasn't looking.

The pressure is growing. The surgery is going fine, everything looks good. The pressure in Paul's gut however is growing by the minute. There is a slight burning sensation with every breath he takes. The dull ache in Paul's gut is slowly building to a sharp pain. Paul feels the sweat bead more heavily on his brow. His abdomen feels swollen and taut, like an overfilled water balloon just waiting to burst. Paul tries to distract himself by checking the living corpse's vitals once again. It does little to help. Everyone else is watching the surgery. Nobody is watching Paul. Nobody can see the distress and discomfort slowly spreading across his face.

"Here it is."

Dr. Philips' tone of triumph is a momentary distraction from Paul's mounting problem. In his hand Dr. Philips holds a section of small intestine, bent over double like a kink in a garden hose. Following the living corpse's previous surgery scar tissue had formed, attaching things in a way they were not meant to be attached. Over time the scar tissue had pulled the two parts of the intestine closer together, creating the obstruction, the kink.

"Scalpel."

Dr. Philips made the find, but as usual Dr. Stone would get the glory. Paul lifts the asked for instrument from the tray. Dr. Stone looks up at Paul for a moment, taking in the broad shouldered, obviously uncomfortable, nurse beside him. Dr. Stone gives a loathing grunt behind his mask. Paul can see the judgement in Dr. Stone's eyes. Another weak willed nurse who can't even handle the sight of another person's innards. What's the medical profession coming to? Paul has no problem with surgeries, an overindulgence in spicy Tex-Mex is another matter. Paul hands Dr. Stone the scalpel, cursing him under his breath.

"Scalpel."

Guts are supposed to slide against each other easily, not stick together. Few people realize how much their insides move around. The kink in the long hose of the intestine is an easy fix. A few quick slices with the scalpel by Dr. Stone's expert hands and the scar tissue is gone. The hose unkinked. The flow of its contents are again unabated. Paul watches with rapt desperate attention as the two surgeons continue running their hands along the intestines, looking for any other possible problems.

The pain increases to truly uncomfortable levels now. Paul feels twinges that try to bend him over double. A silent burp crawls its way up his esophagus, bringing acid and bile with it. Paul quickly swallows it back down. He feels like his insides are a collection of over-inflated balloon animals, twisted into new and painful shapes by a sadistic clown. His body screams for the pressure to be relieved, demands that the foulness be expelled. Paul's mind refuses to give in. This is not the time. This is not the place. He just has to hold on a little bit longer.

Dr. Stone and Dr. Philips finish examining the living corpse's interior. They confer and concur. The one kink was the only problem. It is time to close up the incision and call it a day. Paul has a kernel of hope in his mind. Something to hold onto. Something to keep him going, to keep him fighting his own body

31

for just a little while more. Soon it will all be over. Soon he can make his escape to the privacy of the lavatory where all can be put right with the world. Only a little bit more to go.

"Dr. Philips, would you like to close the patient?"

Dr. Stone's offer to the assisting surgeon is like a death knell in Paul's mind. Dr. Philips is a nice man, probably one of the nicest people in the hospital. Paul has always liked Dr. Philips, but now he is the greatest enemy that Paul has ever had. Dr. Philips works slowly and exactly as he closes up the wound. Every stitch is a work of art, perfectly and evenly placed. Dr. Philips takes pride in his work. He loves nothing more than to see a patient with a barely visible scar. Paul wishes he would hurry, even if it leaves a Frankenstein scar across the living corpse's abdomen.

One by one. Each stroke of the surgical needle pushing through skin and pulling the suture tight seems to take an hour. Paul's hands are clamped in ineffectual fists of rage against forces he knows he cannot beat. Every beep of the EKG is the tick of a count down until his defenses break and the stenches of his bowels can no longer be held back. Paul can feel himself pucker, he can feel the last bits of resistance start to crumble. His face glows red with effort and future shame.

Dr. Philips is on the last suture. There may still be hope. It is the last thought in Paul's mind, the momentary distraction of hope, when the dam bursts. A silent wave of stink forces its way outward into the world, filling the surgery center with its pungent odor. All work stops. Dr. Cohen stands up straight in his corner.

"Good god. What the hell is that stink?"

Dr. Philips looks at Dr. Stone. Dr. Stone looks back at Dr. Philips. Lisa holds her hand near her face, not sure what to do. Wanting to cover her nose, but unable. The EKG machine beeps steadily in the background. Dr. Stone's voice, thick with anger, breaks the silence.

"Shit. We must have pierced the intestine. We'll have to open him back up."

Dr. Stone doesn't bother to ask Paul for the scissors. He reaches over and grabs them himself. The perfect sutures of Dr. Philips are cut away, reopening the body cavity to the world. Paul starts to open his mouth, an admittance of guilt starts to pass through his lips, but is stopped short. The back of Dr. Stone quivers in rage at the unexpected setback. The hospital's best surgeon has been brought low by a mistake normally done by an intern. In his mind's eye all Paul can see is Dr. Stone throwing surgical tools at him, cursing him with terms he never knew existed. Nobody likes Dr. Stone, but he is a man of power and standing, a man who can destroy a career on a whim.

Dr. Stone and Dr. Philips begin to comb their way through the intestines once again. Inch by inch. Looking for a perforation they will never find. The smell in the room is overwhelming. Sulfurous fecal particles climb like a conquering horde into the innocent nasal passages of everyone in the room. Nobody is watching Paul. All eyes are on the pink tubes in the surgeon's hands. All eyes are desperately looking for the hole, that when fixed, will allow them to escape from this horrendous gas chamber.

The escape of the first brings some respite, but it is not enough. A second follows, and then a third. Each just as silent and just as deadly. For Paul the feeling is a mix of shame and ecstasy, relief and horror. Paul opens his mouth behind his mask again, and again closes it, saying nothing. The lack of an initial response has already destroyed any chance of a confession now.

The stench in the room increases and the surgeons double their efforts to locate their mistake. Dr. Cohen walks over and looks over their shoulders, hoping another pair of eyes can end their suffering. Lisa gags dramatically behind her mask, her eyes watering. The living corpse lays on the table, breathing easy, vitals normal, oblivious to the world around it.

Peaches

The woman on stage reached back and with a squeeze of her fingers let her bra fall to the floor. The crowd hooted and cheered. The woman whipped back her blonde hair, curled a leg around the pole, and threw herself into a spin. Leo leaned forward and put a two dollar bill on the rack, then leaned back and crossed his big arms. Leo watched the woman. Devin watched Leo. Her eyes moved across his face. Leo's features betrayed nothing. He uncrossed his arms, took a pull off his beer, and crossed them again. No signs. No emotion. Nothing.

Two dollar bills lined the rack. Here it was always two dollar bills, ones were not allowed. Even more filled the pit. The woman on display was whipping the crowd into a frenzy. Men leered. Lights flashed. Men cheered. The woman knew how to put on a show. She knew how to get what she wanted. Devin looked up and for a moment her eyes locked with those of the woman on display. Deep brown eyes. Devin broke away. It was best not to make eye contact. Eye contact could lead to trouble. Devin didn't want to be drug in. Devin didn't want to be part of the entertainment. Someone had to stay sober. They still had to get home at some time. Devin wasn't near drunk enough for that kind of shit.

Neon lights lined the walls. Beer signs. Evocative figures. Nothing poignant. The neon reflected off the top of Leo's shaved head. Devin smoothed the material of her dress on her lap, white with small blue polka dots. Nice material. It felt good under her hands. A flash of neon reflected off the green jade of her bracelet. White was more expensive, but she liked the color of the green better. A business trip to Taiwan. A trip to the night market. She had haggled the dealer down to half his original price. It had been a good trip. She wished Leo had come to share it.

The crowd started cheering again. The woman's bottoms had dropped off. Devin didn't really see why it was such a momentous occasion. The thong looked more like an eye patch than underwear. Men gaping. Men smiling. Devin looked at Leo again. Her eyes searched his face of stone. Just a little something. The rise of an eyebrow. A slight curl at the corner of his mouth. Nothing. Leo leaned forward, took a drink of his beer, leaned back, scratched his nose, and re-crossed his arms.

Buzzing from her purse on the floor next to her chair. Devin looked around. No one was paying attention, all eyes were on the woman. Devin reached down and plucked her phone from its nest of blue leather. She laid it carefully on her lap. A text.

Hey girl.....where u at?
At Casa Diablo with Leo.
Really?!
Yeah...
Should meetup. Me and Kev going dancing at Crystal.
We'll see.
It's okay to come by yourself.

A hand on her shoulder. A big hand. A strong hand. A flutter in her heart. The ghost of a memory. Devin looked up.

Leo was still in his chair, taking another drink of beer. The bouncer stood behind her, big and imposing, overdeveloped arms and chest in a black t-shirt one size too small. The big man's voice barely carried over the sound of the music and the crowd.

"No cameras."

Devin flashed a girlish smile. Young. Naive. Innocent.

"I'm just texting a friend."

The bouncer's tired eyes pushed through her defensive sortie. Such things had worked better when she was younger. The bouncer repeated his demand.

"No cameras."

Devin looked at Leo. Leo glanced at her, then up at the bouncer, and then back to the woman gyrating in front of him. Devin waited for a moment, giving him a chance. Leo leaned forward and put another two dollar bill on the stage. Devin looked back up at the bouncer.

"Okay. I'm sorry."

She put her phone back in her purse.

"Don't let it happen again."

The bouncer hefted his mass away. Devin looked at Leo and bit her lower lip. Leo ignored her. The woman on the stage scooped up her money and discarded clothing. She sauntered off, a lioness finished with her kill. A new woman took her place. Almond eyes. Black hair down to her waist. Red lace bra and panties. The new woman took a rag and spray bottle from the corner and began to clean the pole. Leo watched. Devin licked her lips.

"That was Katie."

Leo grunted his affirmation.

"She and Kev are going dancing tonight at the Crystal."

Leo grunted again. Devin waited. She could see the gears turning in Leo's head. All she had to do was wait. If it was his idea there could be a chance. Leo's eyes narrowed. His view

moved past the woman rubbing down the pole, past the lights
and the leering people, past the back wall of the club.
Calculations processing. Computations finalizing. Leo's big
shaved head turned towards her. His eyebrows rose a little
higher on his forehead. The words rushed out of Devin's
mouth.

"Maybe we could go to?"

Leo took a drink of his beer, grunted again, and turned back
to the stage. A new song started playing. The new woman
started throwing herself around the pole. Leo's eyes followed
her every move. Devin fingered the hem of her dress. The
material felt nice between her fingers. She took a deep breath in
and let it out. Devin scooted her chair back.

"I'm going to the bathroom."

Leo turned to look at her. Devin reached down, hesitated,
picked up her purse, and rose up from her seat. Leo's eyes
watched her. He lifted a finger and pointed towards the bar.

"Could you get me another beer?"

Devin looked down at Leo.

"Sure."

Leo turned back to the woman on the pole. The woman's red
lace bra fell to the ground. The crowd began to cheer. Leo put a
two dollar bill on the rack. Devin turned and started winding her
way through the tables and chairs. A few glazed gazes broke
from the spectacle before them and followed the roll of her hips.
Devin ignored them. She looked back once. Leo was still
staring at the woman on the pole.

The doors to the bathrooms were marked *Incubus* and
Succubus. Devin pushed in the door marked *Succubus*. The
bathroom was dirty. Grime in the corners. Spotty mildew.
Wadded paper towels, overflowing the garbage can, all over the
floor. Everything looked old and badly used. The lighting was
far too bright, making the dirt stand out all the more. Two
women stood talking opposite the sinks. Two strippers. One

black and one white. The black one stood facing Devin. She wore lingerie in a brilliant lime green. The white one stood facing away in pink undies and a white polka dot bra. Part of her butt crack was sticking out. A tramp stamp crossed from hip to hip, stating *Peaches* in a stylish font. Devin pushed past them, moved into one of the stalls, and shut the door.

Wet toilet paper was stuck to the floor. The stall walls were covered in graffiti, scratches, and layers of paint of varying age. The toilet seat had piss on it. Devin looked for a hook to hang her purse. There was no hook. Devin looked down at the seat and sighed. The ass gasket dispenser above the toilet was empty. Devin ripped off several squares of toilet paper and gave the seat a good rub down. Fuck it. It wasn't like her ass was going to absorb anything. Devin pulled down her panties, hiked up her dress, and sat down with her purse on her lap. On the stall wall, at eye level, just below a dried mass of mucus, someone had scratched *Peaches is a super cunt*. The two strippers talked quietly to each other.

"I scored some snow, you want a bump?"

"I can't. I go on stage soon."

"C'mon. They gave me too much."

"No thanks."

"It's too much just for me."

"Don't do it all then."

"You know I can't take it home. C'mon, do a bump with me."

"I have to go."

The sound of stilettos on tile. The bathroom door opened and closed. Devin coughed and finished her business. She tore off some toilet paper and wiped herself. She pulled back up her underwear and smoothed back down her dress. She didn't want to touch the toilet handle. She flushed it with her foot. Devin took a deep breath and opened the stall door. Peaches was still standing opposite the sinks, biting one of her fingernails. For a second they made eye contact. Peaches was wearing far too much mascara, her lashes thick and clumpy. Devin broke away. She pushed her way past to the sink and started washing her hands. She could see Peaches in the mirror, watching her.

"Hey you?"

Devin shut off the water and turned around.

"Yeah?"

"Do you want a bump?"

Devin licked her lips.

"What?"

"Do you want a bump?"

"No thank you."

Devin moved towards the door. Her hand worked the paper towel dispenser. She tore off the paper towel and dried her hands. Peaches watched her.

"I don't have a problem you know."

Devin turned slightly back towards Peaches.

"I don't have a problem you know. I just have too much for just me and I can't take it home."

Devin threw the paper towel into the trash. It rolled off the overflowing pile and onto the floor. Peaches sniffed and watched.

"I don't have a problem."

"Okay."

Devin turned and left the bathroom. The door swung closed behind her. Devin could feel Peach's eyes burrowing through the door. She took a deep breath and let it out. She went to the bar and ordered a beer. She paid with a twenty. The bartender gave her the glass and seven two dollar bills. The black woman from the bathroom was cleaning the pole, getting ready for her set. Devin felt her phone vibrate. The bouncer stood by the door, watching everything. Leo lounged back in his chair, eyeing the woman wiping down the pole. His face was blank, no sign of anything. Devin put the glass of beer to her lips, spit in it, swirled the liquid with her finger, and headed back to the empty seat next to Leo.

The Champion

The line was a lot shorter than Salt and Straw, fewer tourists, so it had that going for it. Otherwise it looked just about the same as its more popular cousin. The big glass topped freezer filled with cartons open for the world to see, filled with a plethora of small batch colors and flavors. The metal tasting spoons, handles up in their container. The iPad used in place of a cash register, the use of physical money heavily frowned upon. There are only so many ways to differentiate ice cream once you reach a certain quality. There was no good reason to stand in a longer line just to claim allegiance to a certain name.

Lisa stared down at her phone, texting and Facebook messaging a constant unending stream of shares and likes. Was she checking them in? Probably. Who was she talking to now? God only knew. It was really none of his business. Paul stood behind her in line and let his eyes wander across Williams Avenue, his vision blurred by the brightness of the setting sun, darkened only by the shadows of trees and power poles. There wasn't much to see on the block, just the condominiums above the shop and the Life Change Christian Center across the street. People didn't prowl the sidewalks here in large numbers like they did in the enclaves of hipsterdom scattered across the city. Here it was still peaceful. Its time had not yet come.

They were coming though. You couldn't have a business that used terms like 'local' and 'artisanal' and not expect them to come. The young man in front of them was the perfect example. His hair was gelled and swept back, his horn rimmed glasses slightly askew, white v-neck t-shirt, and jeans baggy around the ass but skin tight around the legs. Paul didn't really understand the sense of a fashion that gave men the look of a frog being held up by its front feet, but then again, Paul didn't really understand much about fashion anyway. No one would ever say that he was on the forefront of male style trends. Running shirt, cargo shorts, and sandals could hardly be called a look. Such places weren't Paul's favorite haunts, but Lisa liked them, so he was along for the ride.

The young man in front of them took his sweet ass time picking out a flavor. He felt the need to try a spoonful of every single one. Lisa typed away on her phone. Paul felt like he should try and start a conversation. They used to talk all the time. Nothing of interest came to mind. Such was marriage. He contented himself calculating the percentage of patrons in the shop who were wearing flannel. Fifty-five percent. The ceiling fans turned in their slow arcs. The young man made his purchase, a single lonely scoop in a white bowl, and moved aside. Lisa didn't notice, her eyes remained locked on her phone. Paul reached out and gave her a light prod on her lower back. She looked up, glanced back annoyed, and then moved forward.

Lisa took her time. Following her predecessor's lead, she asked for a taste of several options that peaked her fancy. Paul waited and studied the menu on the wall above the counter. Thrilla in Vanilla, Cortadito, Bananas Foster, Butterscotch

Blondie, Maple Jack Bacon Brittle, Sweet Corn, Peaches and
Scream, and Chocolate. The names all seemed to run together.
Nut-free options, gluten-free options, and vegan options too.
Made with coconut instead of milk. Several contained one type
or another of liquor. Lisa moved aside, two scoops of Brown
Butter Almond Brittle in a white bowl, and walked outside to
find a table al fresco. Paul stepped forward.

The girl behind the counter had bleached blonde hair shaved
on one side. The frames of her Buddy Holly glasses were a
bright green and her lips were painted firetruck red. Piercings
adorned one eyebrow and her nose. Half inch spacers sat in both
ear lobes. Her eyes gave a steady impression of disdain which
made Paul feel a strange sense of shame for daring to bother her.
The guilty feeling made Paul's hackles rise. The girl stared at
him, it made him nervous. He averted his gaze back upwards to
the menu. The woman gave out an audible sigh.

"Do you know what you'd like?"

Paul glanced at her a moment, then returned to the safety of
the options written above her head.

"Just looking."

"Perhaps you'd like to try a few?"

"No, just give me a second."

The girl rolled her eyes. Paul pretended not to see. He
glanced back out the door, past the people waiting in line behind
him. Lisa sat at an outside table, playing with her phone. The
girl in front of him tapped her finger on the counter. Paul turned
his head to a dirty look. His eyes scanned across the menu.
Mint Chunk, Lychee Coconut, Mango, Burnt Sugar. Someone
behind him in line coughed into their hand. People shifted from
one foot to the other. Paul's eyes locked onto the bottom of the
menu.

"What's the Mondo Challenge?"

"It's three pounds of ice cream plus all the toppings. You
couldn't handle it."

Paul's teeth clenched and his neck muscles tightened. The girl stared down her nose at him, examining the square peg in the round hole. Paul stared back. Her eyes were green.

"I'll take that."

The girl rolled her green eyes, turned, and got a large bowl off the shelf behind her.

"You get to pick three flavors."

Paul's eyes ran across the list of flavors again. Now was not the time to delay. Now was the time to be bold.

"Bourbon Toffee, Chocolate, and Basil Blueberry."

The girl rolled her eyes again, laid the bowl on a scale, and started scooping. The cartons of Bourbon Toffee and Chocolate were both half gone. The Basil Blueberry was still almost completely full. Tan, brown, and blue scoops filled the bowl. Two large bananas were peeled, sliced, and added. Then came large dollops of hot fudge, caramel, and toffee. Followed by a mound of whipped cream, sprinkled with nuts and topped with a cherry. The girl shoved a spoon into the concoction and plopped it down on the counter in front of Paul.

"That will be twenty-seven-fifty."

"I'm getting the woman ahead of me too."

"I know."

Paul swiped his card and signed his name with his finger. The signature sort of looked like his. He picked up his overflowing bowl and carried it outside to the table. The people in line stared at the monstrosity in his hands as he walked past. Lisa was still on her phone. Half of her ice cream was already eaten. Her spoon slowly carved off delicate slices that she let melt in her mouth. Paul dropped his bowl on the table with a loud thud that vibrated the metal top. Lisa looked up, annoyed, and then her eyes fell on the frozen beast on the table in front of Paul.

"What the hell is that?"

"The Mondo Challenge."

"Are you seriously going to eat all that?"

Paul sat down and shrugged.

"The girl behind the counter didn't think I could do it."

Lisa gave Paul a long measured look, her mouth flat and her brow furrowed. She turned and looked at the girl behind the counter, busily scooping ice cream for the next customer in line. Lisa turned her gaze back to Paul. She stared for a moment, gears cranking in her brain. She started to say something, stopped herself, started again, and stopped herself again. Giving out an audible sigh she returned to tapping at her phone.

Paul shrugged again, and started his attack. Each spoonful was carefully crafted, containing ice cream, banana, topping, and whipped cream. Alone they were nothing. All together they were heaven. The Blueberry Basil was disgusting. With the first bite Paul regretted his decision to add it to the mix. At first he avoided it all together, but then thought better of it since he didn't want to have to finish it all at the end. He then started eating just it in an attempt to clear it out first thing, but it was difficult to choke down spoonful after spoonful. Finally, he set himself to the strategy of rotating each spoonful to a different flavor. Spoonful after spoonful. Head down. Arm shoveling. A steady unending pace of ice cream. A third of the bowl disappeared in short order. Paul looked up from his bowl, feeling proud of his accomplishment so far. He glanced over at the girl behind the counter. She was wiping down the glass top. He turned and looked at Lisa who glanced up from her phone to meet his eye and then look down at his bowl.

"How's the blue one?"

"Not that good."

"Can I try a bite?"

Paul stopped with his spoon half raised.

"No."

Lisa paused. She looked annoyed.

"C'mon, just one little bite."

Paul's free hand protectively cupped the large bowl.

"If I let you have a bite then I won't complete the challenge."

Lisa's eyebrows rose high on her forehead.

"Really Paul? Really?"

Paul shrugged his shoulders.

"It's a challenge."

Lisa rolled her eyes, sat back in her chair, and stared out at the traffic rolling past. Her phone lay on the table, screen down so Paul couldn't see it. Paul put the spoonful of ice cream in his mouth and grimaced. Blueberry Basil again. The girl at the counter took an empty carton out from under the glass and replaced it with a new full one. Paul spooned more ice cream into his mouth. Lisa refused to look at him. She was mad. Her mouth was held tight the way it always was when she was angry. That would be trouble later. It would be best to diffuse the situation. The bowl of ice cream was halfway finished. Paul halted his spoon arm, and looked up at his wife.

"Who have you been talking to?"

Lisa looked at Paul out of the corner of her eye.

"Phoebe."

Paul licked his lips, still sweet with ice cream.

"How is she doing?"

Lisa turned to face Paul and leaned forward, resting her elbows on the table.

"Oh my god. You would not believe what her boyfriend has been up to. The other evening, he went out drinking with his friends all night. Never called once. Didn't get home until three in the morning, covered in stripper glitter. Phoebe was furious. I guess he wouldn't even..."

Paul stared at Lisa's mouth, watching her lips move, but not really hearing the words. Phoebe was not really his favorite person. She was overly sensitive and could be a real bitch. Paul had never met her boyfriend, the latest in a long line suckered in by Phoebe's good looks. Paul gave the occasional nod of his head or grunt of affirmation or derision to show that he was listening. Slowly his hand moved down and dipped his spoon into his bowl. The spoon rose and the ice cream disappeared into his mouth. The cycle was repeated, a little quicker than the first, then again, and again. A steam engine gradually picking up steam. Paul kept his eyes on Lisa's moving mouth. The flash of teeth. The flick of her tongue. The mound in the bowl shrank to a third of its original size.

The phone on the table buzzed. Lisa broke off mid-sentence, picked it up, released a short snort, and started typing back a reply. Paul lowered his head and concentrated his efforts. Each spoonful was harder than the last. The taste of cream was sickly sweet on the back of his tongue. His stomach twisted at least a quarter turn, overflowing with frozen dessert. He was a runner sprinting towards the finish. Just a bit more. Just a bit more to the end. A sharp pang stabbed through his belly. Pressure built in his gut, demanding release. Maybe he could push it through quietly. No, this was something substantial, more solid. Only five more bites to go. Now four. He just needed to hold out a little more. No. There was no waiting. The time was now. The ice cream could wait. He could do what needed to be done and then finish the Mondo Challenge. No harm. No foul. The two were unrelated.

"I have to go to the bathroom."

Lisa looked up and then directed her eyes back onto her phone. Paul got up from his seat, his ass clenched, and went back inside the shop. He pushed his way past the line of people to the pair of bathroom doors. One was marked Cups and the other was marked Cones. The window next to the knob of the one marked Cones was red. The window next to the one marked Cups was green. Single holers with a lock. No reason to stand on ceremony. Besides, things were on the move. Paul went into the one marked Cones and locked the door. A quick swipe with toilet paper ensured a clean seat. Down went Paul's pants and his life got a lot more comfortable.

Paul had a gut full of dairy on top of a large lunch and a couple beers after work. He knew that he should have seen this one coming. It didn't matter though. Soon he would be back outside. Soon he would be eating the last four bites. He would scrape the last stray bits of melted ice cream out of the bottom of his bowl. Hell, maybe he'd even lick it clean. He'd carry it back to the counter. His back would be straight. His shoulders raised. His arms and legs cockily swinging in perfect time. He'd put the bowl on the counter, just hard enough to make it audible. The girl behind the counter would see him do it. She'd know the he had done it. Paul could see her face. She'd know that she had been wrong. She'd realize what kind of a man Paul was. Paul would strut back outside. He'd take the arm of a swooning Lisa and move on down the street, never once looking back.

Paul cleaned up and started to stand and pull up his pants. Another sharp pang ripped across his gut. His pants went back down. He really should have known better. Three pounds was a lot to add to the system. Someone knocked on the door. Paul ignored it. Things were going to take a while. The minutes ticked by. Paul kept his mind on the business at hand. Only four more bites. Maybe the girl would think he was in the bathroom puking. That wouldn't be fair. His current issue was unrelated. His frozen cargo was still all in place. Screw her if she did. He would know the truth.

Paul cleaned himself and rose up again. He felt at ease. Relaxed. Another knock sounded at the door. Paul washed his hands and dried them, waving his hand twice below the automatic dispenser to get enough paper towel. He looked at himself in the mirror and smiled. Four more bites. Just four more bites to go. Paul opened the door, a woman stood on the other side. She looked at him, then at the sign on the door, then back at him again. The woman's eyes narrowed and her mouth began to move. Paul pushed past her. The girl behind the counter and the people waiting in line and sitting at the tables all watched him. Paul lowered his head and moved towards the door. The people in the shop went back to what they were doing before.

Lisa sat at the metal table outside, still clacking away on her phone. The table was empty except for a small dollop of blue ice cream where his large bowl had once been. Paul stood over the empty table, staring down at nothing.

"Where's my ice cream?"

Lisa looked up.

"What?"

"Where's my ice cream?"

"I thought you were done. I took it to the counter."

Paul turned his head and looked at the girl behind the counter. She was filling a cone for a kid. She stopped for a moment and looked back. Their eyes met. The girl went back to filling the cone. Paul turned his gaze back towards his wife.

"But I was only four bites from completing the challenge."

"What in the hell are you talking about Paul?"

Lisa stared at Paul. His hands clenched and unclenched. His back teeth clamped down tighter. Lisa looked down at her phone, finished her message, and put it in her bag. She rose slowly from her seat, a cat stretching in the sun.

"You ready to go?"

Paul nodded weakly. Lisa started walking towards the car. Paul turned to follow, stopped, and looked at the girl behind the counter one last time. She was polishing the glass counter again. She did not look up. Lisa stopped walking and turned around.

"Paul, you coming?"

"Yes dear."

Lisa turned and started walking again. Paul followed meekly behind.

A View of Paradise

My pace is brisk. It's cold outside. My breath billows in front of me, bringing to mind the movements of an old steam train. Like the train my course is set and I don't deviate from my path. Throngs of people surround the fenced in tents where Pioneer Square once stood. Some chatter excitedly, glad to be done with another work day. Ready to start their evenings of debauchery and cheer. Ready to unwind and pretend that their worries and sorrows don't exist. Some stagger awkwardly. They've been here longer. Early conquerors who no longer fear their problems. No, the only problems they face now are finding a place to eat, getting home to fall asleep in their own beds, and avoiding puking on the street. They yell in loud voices to be heard over the din, both the clamor from the Winter Alefest, and the ruckus within their own heads.

I walk around the edge of the guarded fortress, its chain link walls keeping the celebration from spreading beyond the confines of the square. The entrance is guarded by volunteers and hired security. A line of people slowly shuffle their way forward into the promised land. I lean against a tree, its bows bare, its green leaves long turned yellow and fallen. I send a text letting her know where I'm waiting. My phone vibrates in my pocket. She's on the Max and on her way. Kevin and Lisa are with her.

I feel tense. Why do I feel so tense? My back is stiffer than it should be. My shoulders tight. I look forward to seeing her, but I also worry about when she arrives. Will this be a good day or a bad day? She's actually agreed to come out and do stuff with me. This points towards it being a good day, but one can never tell. It's impossible for me to guess until I actually see her. It's been awhile since we've had a good day. I can hardly remember what it feels like. My hand runs through my hair and pauses at my temples. In my mind's eye I can see the gray. The gray that wasn't there a few months before.

For just a moment, a brief moment, a thought echoes through my brain. You can't do this anymore. There's nothing you can do. This is a monster you can't fight. The end is already written in stone. I tremble. The crowds around me seem to close in tighter without moving. I wish I were anywhere else. I begin to feel afraid. They can see. They can all see.

I force my thinking away from the internal. I will my body back under control. My shoulders relax. These thoughts help nothing. These images only hurt, they don't help. I gaze out at the people around me. I study the world, the exterior, a distraction from the internal, the pain. I try to commit every detail to memory. The denizens of Portland, the world of the weird. The variety of the city moves all around me. Bustling by in its constant anthill motion. I'm stationary, a part of the tree that I lean on. I'm a solitary point in a world of movement.

Across the street a group of freegans sit. They all wear worn out clothes in shades of green and brown. Their greasy hair is knotted into unwashed dreadlocks, white Rastafarians, only with none of the pride or tradition. All have at least three piercings.

Ears, nose, lips, and god only knows what else. One has a small dog on a string. The dog is dirty and flea ridden, much like its master, but at the very least looks well fed and happy to see everyone around it. The freegans regard the world with haughty disdain, mirroring the expression that I'm undoubtedly carrying on my own face as I look at them.

I don't like the freegans. My dislike for them makes for a good distraction, a safe avenue for my thoughts to go. The vast majority of them don't have to live the way they do. They have chosen to. They've chosen to live outside of what they view as a cruel and heartless modern society. They're the extreme of a narcissist generation taught that everything they do is special. The reality of the world is too harsh for them, too unfair, so it must be that the world is wrong. The freegans sit in the street and aggressively panhandle. They dig through fast food dumpsters and eat the food we throw away. They think they're free, not part of the capitalist machine. The freegans are not free. They survive on the waste and leftovers of our society. They depend on it for survival, but do nothing to contribute. They're parasites.

One of the freegans pulls out a newer model phone. It's unusual to see a group of freegans this time of year. Normally by now most have headed south to warmer climates, or have returned to their parents' upper middle class homes. I don't mind the freegans for their beliefs. I mind them because they have so much, and take from those who have nothing. Every quarter they panhandle, every soup kitchen they visit, every shelter bed they occupy, is one less for those who are homeless and truly unable to do any better for themselves. The true detritus of society. The freegans are able, they're just unwilling.

I see Helen walking towards me, a tall figure in the crowd getting off the Max. She's framed in the streetlights, her two friends in tow. I force myself to banish my worries into the nether regions of my mind. I force myself to stand up straight, to raise my hand and wave, to smile. She sees me and a big smile spreads across her face. She waves back excitedly and her pace quickens. I feel my muscles relax somewhat. My grin widens a bit, less forced than it was. I feel a warm wave pass through my being. What is the word for it? What is the word for this feeling? This evening is going to be all right. It's going to be a good day.

We hug as we meet each other, holding on a little longer. A comfort. I say hello to Kevin and Lisa. As always Kevin is fairly quiet, subdued behind his thick beard. Lisa is the main source of communication from the two of them. Helen looks beautiful as she always does. Her tall body encased in her cream colored coat with a fringe of fake fur along the collar and hood. Her head covered by a crocheted winter cap that she made herself. We get into line and make small talk as it slowly snakes forward, chatting about our days with their various joys and tribulations.

I find myself watching her. Listening to the tone of her voice. Eyes appraising her posture and every movement. Watching for the signs of trouble that I've become so accustomed to. Wary of the difficulty and hurt that's boiled down to a single word. Anxiety I've heard her mutter it too often. An excuse for all that has gone wrong. I'm scared of the monster rising up again. Scared that at any moment she'll slip away again into the depths. She can feel me watching her. She takes my hand and gives it a squeeze. My somber face brightens and I smile.

We get to the entrance and pay our money for plastic mugs and drink tickets. The tented square is crowded. It's impossible to move without pushing other people out of the way. A mass in constant motion. A pack of penguins, jostling one another to avoid being on the cold outer edges. The heat of a thousand

bodies warms the tent to room temperature. The noise of a
thousand conversations is deafening in the enclosed space.

Lisa and Kevin see another couple that they know and stop to
say hello. I take Helen's hand and lead her off into the crowd to
join one of the long snaking lines to sample a beer. She's
smiling. It feels so good to see her smiling. I smile back. Her
eyes are twinkling. How long has it been since I last saw her
eyes twinkle? She's so beautiful. All of it's been worth it.
Every bit of pain and every bit of hurt. It's all been worth it.
There are no doubts in my mind. No worries. I'm just here. I'm
just now.

Signs cover the walls, names of a hundred different beers.
It's impossible to try them all. We look at the list and yell above
the crowd to hear each other, figuring out what beer to sample. I
put in my opinion, my two cents, but it doesn't matter to me. It
doesn't matter what we're doing. With the negotiations over we
get into the appropriate line and wait. We hold hands and lean in
to yell little jokes into each other's ears. It's hard to hear over
the masses. I have trouble hearing in large crowds. It doesn't
matter. I smile and laugh even though I only catch half of what
she says. She smiles and laughs back. We get to the front of the
line and secure our reward for waiting. Our full mugs in tow we
wander the madness, watching the world around us.

It's still a strange feeling. All of my life I've waited for
something to happen, felt like there was something better out
there. Normally in a large crowd like this my head would be on
a swivel. Looking for prospects and opportunities, the vast
majority of which I would never take. This is a different feeling.
I still walk through the world and watch, but I don't feel like I'm
looking for anything. I'm on an island of calm in a sea of chaos.
The world around us is just a blur.

We run back into Lisa and Kevin, who are still talking with
the other couple. Introductions are made in a quiet corner and
Lisa and Helen slip off to use the bathroom. I'm not good with

small talk, especially with people that I don't really know, but tonight I have no worries. Tonight I'm relaxed. Everything seems to come naturally and easy. When Helen comes back she takes my hand again.

The male half of the new couple leans close to be overheard over the crowd. "So, are you two married?"

The question catches me off guard. It's something that I've never heard before. I'm used to being the third wheel. Being looked at and being seen as part of a couple is still something strange and new. To have someone see something like that in me is shocking. Sudden confusion on what I should do. I keep my face neutral and look at her. She is talking to Lisa and Kevin. I don't know if she's heard the question. A secret thrill runs through me. A tingle of excitement that a stranger could look at the two of us and assume such a thing. I want to yell to the heavens that this is the most amazing woman that I've ever met. I can't say it. It would sound foolish. Saying it would scare her too much. It would only worsen her anxiety. It would only strengthen the monster.

"No," I reply.

It's a wonderful night. It's probably the most wonderful time I've had since returning from Asia, since things all started going wrong. We spend a few more hours at the Alefest and then join the wandering crowds on the street in search of food. When dinner is done, Lisa and Kevin separate and leave with their other friends. I drive Helen back to her house. When we go inside all is quiet. Everyone is already asleep or still gone. We go into her bedroom and follow the same routine that we always have.

"I got you something."

"What?"

"A toothbrush. So you can brush your teeth when you stay the night."

I smile. It's a good sign. It's a good thing. Maybe we are coming out of the wilderness. Maybe the horrors of the past are behind us and we can finally start anew. That feeling again. Something that I've not felt since this whole nightmare began. I strip off my clothes and get into bed. She changes into shirt and shorts and joins me. I hold her close and kiss her. She doesn't pull back. I don't kiss her long. I don't want the monster to come back and ruin this day. I don't want her to go away again. I don't want to push her too soon. It all seems so fragile.

We lay on our sides facing each other, my hand caressing hers. She smiles at me. I look into her eyes, her beautiful ocean eyes, and she doesn't look away. It's her. It's really her. It's as though I'm seeing her for the first time since I got back from Asia. I warm myself upon the rays that her eyes emit. Shackles fall from my wrists. Chains that have held us back for so long seem to crumble. A great weight falls from my back.

Her eyes sparkle and dance in the dim light from the window in the darkened room. She laughs and bells ring within my soul. All is as it once was. No distance, no stiffness, no hesitation, no worried glances, no doubts. Both of us are free. How long has it been? How long has she been gone? How long have I lamented? It seems like a lifetime ago. I can feel myself again. I can feel my heart no longer heavy, my face no longer somber, my eyes no longer dull. Perhaps that was the problem. Perhaps neither one of us could recognize the other anymore. She is right here. Right here in front of me. The distance is gone. The great crevasse has closed. I'm laying here right next to her, all the trials and troubles of the world forgotten.

So much I want to say. So many things coursing through me. I hold them all back. It seems like such a fragile thing. I don't want to lose it. I allow myself just one, just a single question.

"What are you feeling right now?"

Her eyes bore into mine. No storms on the oceans held within.

"Contentment."

I smile. It's been worth it. It's all been worth it. I feel my eyes sag and grow heavy. I don't want to close them. I don't want to lose this moment. I let my eyes close, but only for a second.

My eyes open to morning light splashed across the wall in front of me. My face is still smiling. I roll over. Helen lays next to me. Her back to me, staring out the window at the bare tree branches outside. The pace of her breathing gives away that she isn't asleep.

"Good morning."

She doesn't answer. I reach out and touch her shoulder. I can feel her shaking. Her muscles are tight. I can feel the tension. My heart drops. I feel myself begin to shake with fear.

"Good morning," I hear her mumble.

No force, no conviction, just an automatic reply. I pull on her shoulder and she rolls over and looks at me. Her face is somber and thoughtful. It's etched with pain, sadness, guilt, and fear. I look into her eyes, hoping to see the sparkle that I saw the night before. The dream come true. They're blank. It's as though there's nobody behind them. She's gone again. She has gone away again.

I want to grab her. I want to shake her. I want to yell for her to come back. To please come back. Don't go. I miss you. I miss you so much. There's so much I want to do, so much I want to say, but I do nothing. There's nothing I can do. I can feel the despair on my face. I turn away to hide it as she rolls back over and stares back out the window. I get up, pull on my pants, and go out the door to use the bathroom. I don't want to let her see how much I hurt. It will only make things worse.

Dan The Man

Leo knocked the prerequisite number of knocks and waited the prerequisite amount of time. Nobody home. Somewhere in a side yard a dog barked, high and shrill, some kind of small yap dog. Leo adjusted the package in his grip. It wasn't heavy, just an awkward shape. Narrow in height, but wide and long. Leo scanned the barcode on the box with his handheld computer. The machine thought about it for a moment and beeped. It was okay to leave the package. Leo leaned it against the door and punched in a command. The computer beeped again and gave the all clear. Leo walked back up the sidewalk to his waiting truck. The yard on either side was green and perfectly manicured. The neighbors' yards on either side were yellow, desiccated by the summer sun. A garden gnome coyly watched from beneath a cherry tree. The high sharp yap came again. Tiny paws beat a rhythmic back and forth behind a fence before fading off around the house.

Leo climbed into the big brown panel truck with its yellow logo and put the computer into its adaptor. The next address appeared on the screen. He put on his seatbelt, but left the sliding door open. It was hot out. Leo wore a button down short sleeve shirt and shorts the same color as the truck. The shorts only came down to just below mid-thigh. They were always riding up and a little too tight in the crotch, the seam just a little too snug. Leo cranked the ignition and the truck cranked to life. The yapping raised in volume in response. A small dog was standing next to the side of the house. It looked like a chihuahua. Someone had left a gate open. It was a nice neighborhood. Old growth trees, elms and maples, lined the street, shading well kept homes. Leo hated neighborhoods like this. He always felt like such neighborhoods looked down on him. Leo ground the transmission into submission and put the truck into gear. He checked his mirrors and pulled away from the curb. He was only one house down when he felt the bump.

"Fuck."

It was a small bump on the left rear tire, almost like he hit a small rock or a bit of a pothole. Leo hit the brakes and the truck lurched to a halt. He cut the engine. The rumbling racket of the pistons fell silent.

"Fuck!"

The word was a sharp jab into the late morning peacefulness of the neighborhood. Leo slammed his hand down on the steering wheel and let himself partially collapse in his seat, his head resting on his arms.

"Damn it. Damn it. Damn it."

The curses came out in a steady emotionless litany. He didn't want to get out of the truck. Just a rock. He probably just hit a rock. Nothing to worry about. Leo took in a deep breath and let it out. He took in another, held it, and exhaled slowly. Okay. He was okay. Time to follow protocol. Leo punched a code into the computer. The message went out to dispatch. Leo didn't wait for a response. He unbuckled his seatbelt and climbed out the sliding door. Leo got down onto his hands and knees and stuck his head partway under the truck. Jammed between the back dual tires was a mass of brownish hair, dark liquid dribbling across the vulcanized rubber. Leo scrambled away and puked at the base of an elm tree. He sat on the curb, breathing heavy, snorting errant chunks of vomit out of his sinuses, and spitting to clear the taste of bile from his mouth. The computer in the truck beeped. Leo rose, wiped his mouth with the back of his hand, and climbed back into the truck.

<212, report.>

Leo tapped out his reply.

<Hit dog.>

<At last delivery address?>

<Yes.>

<Follow protocol.>

The thought of touching the mass of fur stuck between the duals made Leo's stomach churn. For a moment he thought he might puke again.

<Unable.>

The seconds ticked by with no reply. Leo wondered if he needed to add more. The computer beeped.

<Follow protocol.>

Stupid fuckers. Hadn't he just said he was unable? Leo angrily stabbed in his response.

<Unable. Stuck in duals.>

The seconds ticked by again.

<Do you need assistance?>

Leo wanted the slam the computer against the dash. Stupid sons of bitches. No shit Sherlock.

<Yes.>

<Wait.>

Leo leaned back in his seat. He let in and out a couple of breaths to calm down. The streets were quiet, most everybody was at work. Two middle aged women jogged by. One waved. Leo avoided making eye contact. A blue bird leaped from a branch and winged its way past the windshield. The seconds turned into minutes. The computer beeped.

<369 en route.>

Truck number 369. Dan the Man. Shit. Of all the drivers with nearby routes, Leo had hoped it wouldn't be Dan, but of course it was the son of a bitch. Hell, Dan probably volunteered. To call him crusty would have been a compliment. Dan was foul mouthed, foul smelling, and foul tempered. He had been a driver for thirty years, and given his general attitude, had hated each of the years at an exponentially growing rate. Dan had grown up on a dairy farm back in the Midwest, exactly where seemed to change with each telling, but he delighted in sharing break room tales of his upbringing to anyone unlucky enough to be within earshot. He loved to see people squirm. His only enjoyment in life seemed to be in the telling of ribald jokes that were not designed for laughter, but only to make the people around him uncomfortable. He'd been written up for a couple of offenses, but his impeccable driving record made all forgivable. When something unpleasant needed to be done, Dan was the one to do it. The man was impervious to outside stimuli.

The two middle aged ladies came jogging back the other way. They gave Leo a strange stare, but kept going. Leo watched them through his side mirror, willing them to round the corner before Dan and his antics arrived. He checked the clock on the computer. Eleven o'clock. Shit. He'd been stopped for close to half an hour. Leo was never going to catch up. He was going have to work late. A couple cars came down the street, paused, and moved past. One driver hung his arm out the window, middle finger outstretched. Leo ignored him. A second brown truck came down the road towards Leo's. The driver tootled his horn and pulled to a stop next to the curb across the street. Dan jumped out and started across. Leo got out to meet him.

Dan's brown shirt was unbuttoned one button lower than regulation. He was a thin man, all bones and angles, bald except for a halo of black hair that stretched from ear to ear. A permanent five o'clock shadow that no razor could swipe from existence graced his clenched jaw. His beady eyes were narrowed against the sunlight. His movements were stiff and awkward, a marionette with over tightened strings. Leo was a head taller than Dan, but he always felt intimidated by the man. The two met in the middle of the street. Dan snorted and spit a loogie at Leo's feet, forcing him to take a step back.

"Dispatch said you have some kind of dog problem?"

The voice was gravelly. A mixture of gargled vodka and push pins.

"Yeah."

Leo's voice sounded weak in his ears. A touch higher than normal.

"Couldn't take care of it yourself?"

The tone was filled with contempt which set Leo's teeth on edge. It was the tone used by a friend of the family, maybe your father's drinking buddy. Somebody, given the familiarity, you felt you should impress, but someone who was under no familial obligation to make a little worthless shit feel good about themselves.

"No."

Dan eyed Leo and spit again. The slight curl of a smirk at the edge of Dan's mouth told Leo how much the other man was enjoying watching him squirm. Leo couldn't get himself to look Dan in the eye. Nose and mouth seemed a safer bet, though the occasional glance at the ground was needed even for them. Dan stunk of sour body odor and cinnamon gum.

"Well, let's take a look princess."

Dan moved towards Leo's truck. Leo was forced to scramble after.

"Back left."

Dan moved around the side of the truck, crouched, and stuck his head under by the duals. Dan kept his head down for several seconds, mumbling to himself and poking at the out of sight mass with a single index finger.

"Well, I've got bad news Leonardo."

Leo's muscles tightened.

"What's that?"

"Little fuckers dead."

Dan let out a rumbling laugh deep in his throat. Leo thought about picking up a rock and bashing Dan in the back of the head. He restrained himself. Dan growled and poked between the tires again.

"You really got the son of a bitch wedged in there."

"Can we just get him out please."

Dan pulled his head out, stood up, and stretched his back. His eyes roved across the scene, falling at the base of the elm tree.

"That your breakfast?"

The hands at Leo's sides tightened into fists.

"I need to get back onto my route."

"Calm down murderer. These things happen."

Dan spit towards the elm tree and a hand wiped the sweat from his sunburnt brow.

"You got any garbage sacks in your truck?"

"Yeah, probably."

"Well don't just stand there, go get me one."

The barked command set Leo's legs into motion like a well trained soldiers. He clambered into his truck and rooted around for a bit before coming back with a black trash bag. He handed the bag gingerly over to Dan who snatched it away. The older man eyed Leo up and down, taking him all in. Dan held the bag up, gesturing with it towards Leo.

"Last chance to take care of this yourself pussy willow."

Leo tried again to meet the older man's eye. He wanted to grab the bag. He wanted to shove Dan's words back into his mouth. He wanted to make the bastard shut up. For a moment he thought about reaching for the bag, but the vision of touching the once yapping form wedged between the tires made the back of his throat burn. Leo stared down at the brown shoes on Dan's feet.

"Just take care of it."

Dan's smirk grew bigger and then faded back to its normal level. He sat on the pavement next to the truck, wrapped one hand with the bag, reached his wiry arm up between the duals, and gave a sharp yank. The organic sound of crunching bone and compressing tissue forced vomit into Leo's mouth. He desperately swallowed it back. Some kind of thick liquid dribbled down the inside of the tire to the asphalt. Dan pulled the mass down, turning the ends of the bag inside out, hiding the furry remains from view. He stood, holding the bag at arms length. Leo felt a hard lump at the bottom of his stomach. Dan gestured with the bag.

"Take care of it."

"What do you want me to do with it?"

Dan rolled his eyes.

"Jesus. You hit it. You take care of it. Follow the fucking protocol."

Leo took the bag, careful to hold it as far away from his body as possible. It felt heavier than it should. Leo walked towards the house where he had delivered the awkward package. He stopped and looked back. Dan was leaning against Leo's truck, waiting impatiently. Leo turned back and marched at a near run across the perfectly manicured lawn. He went up to the front door. He knew nobody was home, but the protocol required him to knock. He wrapped on the door in quick succession. God, what if someone was home now? What if they had been on the crapper the first time? Leo's whole body was shaking. He

67

counted out the seconds in his head. Nothing. He knocked again. One...two...three. Nothing. He laid the bag down next to the package and retreated. The cheerful gnome beneath the cherry tree seemed to wink at him. Dan waited until Leo got back next to the truck.

"Anybody home?"

"No."

"Did you leave a note?"

"No."

"That's fucked up. That's real fucked up. What kind of person just leaves a dead dog in a garbage bag by someone's front door?"

Leo climbed into his truck, found a pad and paper, and scribbled out a quick note. He wasn't sure what to say, so he just explained the situation and ended it with an apology. He was feeling nauseous again. Dan read over the note and handed it back.

"It's no Hallmark, but it will have to do. Hurry up and tape it to the door."

Leo obeyed the command, his movements stiff and hurried. He felt like he had drank too much coffee. The world was a vibrating blur. Careful to give the trash bag a wide berth, he taped the note to the door and rushed back. This time the gnome seemed to be scowling, judging eyes following his every movement. Dan waited next to the truck, whistling a tune that sounded like something only in his own head. He took a package of gum out of his pocket, unwrapped a piece, and popped it into this mouth. The tin foil fell to the ground. The sight of Dan handling the gum with the same hand he had used to yank free the dog made Leo's stomach turn. Dan stuck out the pack, offering Leo a piece. Leo shook his head. Dan shrugged and put the gum back in his pocket.

"You deliver that package on the stoop?"

Leo nodded his head."

"Wouldn't it be fucked up if it was a dog bed or something?"

Dan laughed again deep in his throat. The red gum snapped between his teeth. Leo felt sick. He imagined his fist connecting with Dan's mouth. Dan stretched his back again.

"Welp, times a wasting, better get back to work."

Dan moved across the street and got back into his own truck. The truck's engine belched to life. Dan put it in gear, tootled his horn, and drove away. Leo watched him go. It was hot out, but not so hot that his shirt and shorts should be soaked in sweat. A bird chirped. A car drove by. The computer in Leo's truck beeped. Leo climbed back into his truck.

<212, 45 minutes behind schedule.>

Leo breathed in deep and let it out. He cranked the ignition. The engine started. He hit a button on the computer. The next stop was five blocks away. Leo put the truck into gear, checked all his mirrors three times, and headed down the street. Forty-five minutes behind schedule. It was going to be a long day. Leo's mouth still tasted like puke. He wished he had taken the gum.

Probably Crazy

It was while slicing a five day old steak to add to my morning scrambled eggs, between wondering if my consumption of said steak would lead to gastrointestinal problems, that I decided that indeed she was probably crazy. It was not a verdict upon which I came lightly, but rather a full rumination of the evidence which left little doubt in my mind that I was involved in a situation in which it would likely be best to extract myself from post haste. Of course, this was not the first time such a serious thought had crossed my mind. The first moment had been the night before as we made out in my Ford Focus before heading back to the east side of the river, bringing to conclusion our second date and our second night of knowing each other.

"Feel free to say no, but I want to give you road head. I've never done it before and I'd like to do it."

I of course obliged.

While I'm certainly not trained or licensed in the science of psychology, or any of the other brain related studies, I most certainly do have experience in such imbalances of the mind.

Crazy women are to men what assholes are to women; the characterization, not the orifice; and much of my dating years have been spent in the company of women who could probably never be part of the control group of any mental experimentation. I've been hated and I've been loved, all within the course of a single hour. I've seen the highs and lows, the tears and laughs, the soft coos and the spitting anger. I've seen the vanishing of the mind into the deep recesses of the body until all life disappears from the eyes. I've watched anxieties pull loved ones out to sea while they insist that everything is fine, the tide tugging them further out with every word. I've woken up to gibberish in the night and had my house broken into on two separate occasions by a jilted lover. For me, crazy have been a way of life for some time, and I often come upon it, even when actively trying to avoid it.

My means of weight and measure does not stop at those with which I frolic in the heady gardens of Eros' heated lusts. My experience in such matters is every bit as personal as interpersonal, and it is my own three year stint of madness which forms the foundation of my ability to spot the crazy ones. We can always recognize our own. Three years is a long time to be eaten by bouts of anxiety and despair as one dreams of past love and stormy seas that will never be again. To sit and pine away in forgotten sacrifice may seem noble and divine, but that's only from the outside looking in. Personally, I'd rather have the movie of my life be a comedy rather than a tragedy. It may never win an Oscar, but I get to be happy at the end. People who say they would rather live an interesting life rather than a good one, have most likely never lived an interesting life.

I ignored the early signs, not sure if they were actually there or perhaps just creations of my own over anxious mind. I had only recently regained my own sanity, banishing the wishful from the reality, the creation from the actual, but wasn't yet sure how complete the expulsion had been. I was not yet ready to fully trust my faculties to such tasks. I would like to believe that such confusion will lessen over time. However, it seems more probable that one foot will never be on solid ground.

Her name was Sarah, with an H, which she felt was an important distinction from the other type of Sara whose lazy careless parents had cheated them out of the fullness of life which an extra letter would have undoubtedly provided. To call this a sign of being crazy would be to accuse myself. I have long been involved in the never ending feud between those who spell my name S-H-A-W-N and those who spell it S-E-A-N, so I can appreciate the importance of the distinction, even if I really didn't care. She reminded me of a woman I had dated several years before also named Sara, both physically and mentally, minus the H at the end. This was quite a coincidence, which of course I didn't mention. The comparison to an ex would have only been exacerbated by the former's use of the incorrect spelling. Just for the record, S-E-A-N spells Seen, not Shawn, but I digress.

Sarah with an H was one of the many women whom I've met via online dating, a habit I started after fleeing from a fairly healthy relationship, most likely due to how odd such a situation felt. It's been a heady time of endless possibilities with thousands of futures represented by each individual's profile. It's fair to say that I have long had an unhealthy fear of commitment, which makes the thought of such possible travels preferable to any actual long-term trips. My development in the area of relationships of the romantic kind has undoubtedly been stunted and delayed for reasons too numerous to go into at this time. Suffice to say, I have a natural aversion to commitment and intimacy. Commitment I can do without, but my stance on intimacy is more neutral and changes day to day, requiring thoughts of a more long-term nature.

With online dating, I have a simple but effective strategy to help bring my email to the top of the hundreds received by the opposite sex; most of which I've been told involve either four word sentences, requests to commence immediate plowing, or pictures of abs and nothing else. My strategy is more nuanced, involving picking out a single factoid from the prospective partner's profile and using it as a basis of a joke. While making people laugh may seem very obvious, the trick is of course knowing how far to take it. There's a fine line between hilarious everyman and total weirdo, which is of course different for every single person. Since I have a habit of taking things too far, it should be of no surprise that responses from weirdos have been more common.

I once had a friend suggest that perhaps I was putting too much effort into my endeavors of the online nature. She thought it might be a better use of my time to utilize the four word request for drinks route and dynamite the seas until something floats to the top. I found her advice questionable given that she referred to herself as a long-term online dater, the emphasis of the concern being on the phrase long-term. It also doesn't help that I have been personally involved in the grieving process for several of her such gained past relationships, the nature of my role being handing her a towel to clean my freshly deposited emotional support off her back. Plus, I doubt she fully understood how much I enjoy creating such messages, regardless of response. The goal being more in line with art rather than business.

The message sent to Sarah was based off of the mention in her profile of her present state of looking for new partners in crime. This of course led to the obvious suggestion of planning the crime of the century involving robbing a local nickel arcade in the hopes of netting profits in the range of tens, or even hundreds of dollars. Even at this early juncture I had concerns over her stability, mostly due to a picture with her face contorted in the classic crazy girl look. It's something hard to explain, but easily recognized when you see it. A gaping mouth grin and wide open eyes should put up red flags for anyone in the know. There's just something off putting about it. I don't know about you, but I usually squint when I laugh or smile.

That being said, one piece of evidence hardly makes a case and there was nothing else to suggest that something was truly wrong. So I ignored my single doubt and sent the message. Time passed until it became just another of the many left unanswered and forgotten, but after a little over a week I got an unexpected response, filled with declarations of awesomeness and delight. Plans for a first date soon after followed, and arrangements were made to meet for drinks at the Tugboat, a well known place for libations on the west side just off of Burnside. The week was slow, both personally and professionally, except for a date with a different woman the night before, so it was a welcome distraction.

Now I should probably mention that I'm not good at first dates, or really any dates at all. Most of my relationships of any kind of length have always seemed to start with an early hookup, which then morphs slowly until it is unspokenly decided that some kind of relationship has formed. Such methods, while easy, have undoubtedly resulted in my inability to patiently wait for a connection to form, which is probably why I seem to prefer dating crazy people. For example, the woman I went out with on Wednesday was a second date. The first, while pleasant, was largely forced inquiries about each other's facts and pasts broken by nervous silences, especially on my end. For me, in such situations, being flustered is the norm. The second was just mildly better, though I feel perhaps only on my end. She was a nice woman, just not all that exciting. Her big reveals were that she was part of a feminist book club and liked wearing yoga pants. Not exactly the kind of conversation that really digs down into what makes a person tick.

In comparison, talking with Sarah seemed more like we were old friends catching up, who just so happened to have never actually met. The ebb and flow of the conversation seemed to travel down natural routes without any kind of silence to break the natural rhythm. After a few hours of words and imbibing a few libations I gave her a ride back to her house and parted company without any contact between us beyond our verbal sparring and the promise to join her and some friends to see a movie the next day.

At the point of separation there was no thought of mental evaluation beyond how crazy extroverts seem to the introverted and the differences in west coast and east coast attitudes. She was from New Jersey. You can probably assume which of us was the extrovert. However, after driving home and indulging in a tug, my head upon my pillow began to bring forth some doubts. Namely the fact that in reflection it seemed strange how quickly familiar we had become. Now many people would point out that this should be viewed as a good thing. However, while I agree that it's not a definitive sign of future trouble, all my past experiences have put this hypothesis in doubt. Regardless of the past, I decided to keep it separate from the present, and fell asleep looking forward to the following evening.

The next day at work was long and boring so we'll just skip over all that and get straight to the good part. The movie was at seven at Cinema 21 and it had been agreed to meet at the Pope House for drinks before. The Pope House is a converted domicile which mixes drinks long on ingredients but short on kick. It has the vibe of a place you go when you want to feel pretentious, as though indulging alcohol there somehow makes you better than the people doing it elsewhere. It should come as no surprise that it's most often populated by a multitude of hipsters, college kids, and foreigners in suits. The common ilk of such a place. It might sound unfair to attack the foreign, but you just don't see that many suits in Portland, and they especially stand out in a haunt like the Pope House, representing a rejection of the laissez-faire vibe of the establishment. Of course, to be fair to the Pope House, the same people can be found at practically any location along Northwest 21st Street. It's just that type of area.

I'm not the biggest fan of this zone known as the Alphabet District, not just for its usual pedestrians, but also for its lack of parking. After finding a spot and walking in the rain back and forth several times, I finally asked a convenience store clerk for directions and was pointed to the correct location slightly off the main drag. It was while endeavoring in this search that I found myself following two young hipsters for a time and the contents of their conversation summed up the neighborhood nicely.

"I used to only hang out on 23rd until I found 21st. Now I know what I was missing."

I was glad to find my destination and leave young Lewis and Clark to their exposition on the importance of exploration and their unrealized ignorance of the wider world. If nothing else the Pope House was dry, and I found Sarah and her roommate with the impressively large tits in a back corner, various coats and pieces of clothing draped across the adjoining tables, drying after a wet bike ride across town. After some initial quiet concentration to make a suitable drink choice I was comfortably settled into the group and the flow of conversation. Soon after we were joined by Mr. Simon, a local owner of several private room karaoke places, of a type common in East Asia, and also an acquaintance of in from a running group which we're both a part of. This formerly unknown connection had been made by Sarah and I during our first date, but for him my presence was unexpected. When asked about the particulars for this certain proof of Portland's small town atmosphere, both Sarah and I gave reference to the internet, both seeing this fact as no source for embarrassment.

I'm sure both of us gentlemen were glad to be in the presence of these two ladies, for both were fit and easy on the eyes. While I was there to see Sarah, I must admit that her roommate with the impressively large tits was no slouch herself, and I'd be lying to claim I didn't give her the up and down. Don't get me wrong, my mammary preferences have always been more towards small and shapely, but that doesn't mean I don't put some value in a rack of such prodigious size. Now some people may think me a real piece of work to make such observations of my date's roommate, but it should be mentioned that Sarah was the one who pointed them out to me. This included forcing the roommate to get out her phone to show off a recent family vacation picture from Mexico graced by her presence in a bikini, which she had not posted to Facebook due to a slight miscalculation in bikini top size. It's a hard line to balance on, feeling like you're expected to say something complimentary, but at the same time trying to avoid giving the appearance that you're hitting on your date's roommate. This was accomplished via a joke that the people near her in the photo were not there for familial connection, but rather just trapped in a powerful gravitational field. Laughs of course followed.

The goal of the night was to see the newest movie released by the roommate's favorite director, Mr. Anderson. She styled herself as one of his biggest fans, which given her assets, is a fact someone should alert Mr. Anderson of immediately. The roommate had already procured the tickets which of course added to further confusion when it came time to split the check and make our way to the theater. This problem was only increased by the fact that Mr. Simon only had two dollar bills due to a recent visit to Casa Diablo the night before. Things were sorted out as best they could be, the still damp clothes were gathered up, and our group headed out into the rain.

The theater was just a few blocks down and we made good time during a break in the constant squalls. We lined up, went in, and bought ourselves beers and bags of popcorn dripping with an extra squirt of fake butter which is only given upon request. We found ourselves some seats in the surprisingly empty theater and waited for the show to start. Sarah got up to meet more of her friends outside and give them their tickets. Mr. Simon and the roommate sat and talked about open relationships. The roommate preferred such a lifestyle and was unsure how to find other people who preferred it as well. The other member of her current relationship was more in favor of longer term endeavors, a negative which only added to his poor performance in matters often related to one's bed. It was a fairly interesting topic of conversation. The people who slowly filled the theater around us seemed to agree.

I draped my coat across the three seats next to me to save them for Sarah and her as of yet unseen and tardy mates, putting into practice an unwritten rule for all movie theaters. A couple people wandered back and forth, forlornly looking at the prize seats, hopeful that I would recant my stance. Most I ignored, but a few I gave the evil eye until they moved on to mope somewhere else. Sometimes you're regulated to the sides. It's just better to accept it. Sarah came back with her friends. They were a hipster couple. The guy was more so than the girl, with a big bushy beard and knit cap. Introductions were made all around. I didn't bother to remember their names. As the movie started, Sarah pressed her leg up against mine. About halfway through I was groping her leg in return and then playing handsey. I mostly concentrated on the movie. If you like Mr. Anderson's films you'd probably really like it. If you don't like Mr. Anderson's films you'd probably think it was total crap. I enjoyed the movie.

When the final credits rolled we headed to the bathrooms and then outside to find a place to have another drink. In the men's room there was a man whistling aimlessly the entire time and the older gentleman in line behind me kept making eye contact like he wanted to say something but didn't have the guts to do so. Outside, our party was joined by a seventh member, another Sarah, who had also seen the movie, just from a different seating area. Other Sarah was dressed as if she was going as a hipster to a Halloween party. Thick frame glasses, straight bangs, big sweater, you get the idea. In my opinion she would've been fairly attractive if she utilized a different look, but different strokes for different folks I guess.

We first walked across the street to the Gypsy and discovered that it had closed permanently. This seemed rather devastating to Other Sarah, but no one else seemed to care. We next tried a karaoke club owned by Mr. Simon. There were no available rooms. I guess it could be considered a good thing for him, but it was not much use to the rest of us. While the women calculated our next move, Mr. Simon and I stood around making ironic comments about how much his place of business sucked, at least until real customers started walking in. After that it was decided that it would be best for us to leave. On the plus side, the hipsters in our group all seemed quite impressed to learn that they were in the presence of the owner of such a hip business. Our footsteps next took us to North 45, yet another pretentious bar overflowing with people I would never hang out with if left to my own devices. The bartender was nice enough. He remembered my name after my first drink. I can't remember his name so we'll just call him Levi.

The group slowly started to dissolve from there. The hipster couple left to go pick up a friend at the airport and soon after Mr. Simon and the roommate left as well, leaving me sitting at the bar with Sarah and Other Sarah. I sat lazily sipping cider, enjoying a comfortable buzz, as the two ladies complained about how, at least compared to east coast people, west coast people rarely talk to strangers at bars. I was non-committal on the topic. Things became more interesting for a time when Other Sarah went into great detail about how her two goals for the year were being able to achieve female ejaculation and learning to play the drums. She was taking a class to educate herself on one, and had found a music book and drumsticks at the Goodwill to aid in the other. Unfortunately, the drums won prominence and my companions' conversation soon fell off to discussing Other Sarah joining a band Sarah was once part of called the Tri-Sarah-Tops, cleverly named since it was made up of three women named Sarah. The fact that one Sarah had quit years ago and the chance of getting it started again were abysmally low did not seem important and they both soon became enraptured with the topic.

Uninterested in two thirty year old women planning the future of their non-existent band, I sat silently with a new cider expertly provided by Levi and studied the rows of liquor bottles behind the bar. Sarah would occasionally put her arm around me as she spoke and I returned the gesture by occasionally rubbing her leg. Clues were starting to mount and part of me was starting to wonder if I should just vacate her presence in as timely a manner as politely possible. Things felt much too comfortable, as though this had been the present state of things for several years, rather than her being someone I had met just the day before.

Levi kept my glass full as needed, but was far too busy to provide any meaningful conversation, which was fine because I was okay without it. I always have difficulty hearing people in crowded bars. Hence, my common shift towards silent revelry in such situations. I'm either hard of hearing or my hearing is too sensitive, I haven't yet decided which. A man in a suit jacket and his trophy wife sat down on my other side and made a few forays towards starting small talk. They must have been from the east coast. I was polite enough, but being from the west coast, fended off their attempts with grace and ease. By grace of course I mean I was slightly drunk and unable to string together sentences of any wit due to the plethora of internal dialogue moving through my mind. They seemed happy enough talking to one another, so I kept to my study of the bottles behind the bar and the waitress whose sole function at the establishment seemed

to be to stick out her ass when she climbed a ladder to retrieve
the higher up ones.

The night grew late and it was decided to head home. Sarah
had ridden her bike from the east side and, since it was on my
way, I offered to load it in the back of my Ford Focus and drive
her home. This was achieved by folding down the car's backseat
and removing the bike's front tire. However, first I had to locate
my car, which took a little longer than expected, especially given
the continued heavy rain. After completing all operations, I
started the car, and while we waited for it to warm up, we
commenced to making out as one does in such situations.
Things got pretty heated which led to the statement which I
mentioned earlier, which fully brought forth my concern
regarding the sanity of the situation, but of course, who would
really say no to such a request.

Now perhaps she wasn't crazy, but rather a woman filled
with lust, brought forth by my manly musk and skills. I will not
deny that in matters of mouth to mouth connection, I'm not
without a certain level of proficiency. My secret is to match my
partner's level of tongue and throw in the occasional ear nibble
for good measure. Complaints of the sexual kind are rarely
levelled against me, except for early on during my college years
when a single night's companion voiced her lack of satisfaction
with my efforts, her a woman of experience equal to thirty
men. Some people might let such a proclamation bring them
down, but not me. After all, the only thing it definitively proved
was that out of the three and a half billion men on this planet,
thirty at that given time were definitely better than me.

It was a strangely erotic and uncomfortable drive of
approximately ninety blocks, from west to east across the
Burnside bridge. I've never been good at multitasking and it
stretched my concentration to the limit, what with the prudent
careful nature of my turning, braking, and accelerating to avoid
accidental damage down below. Eye contact with my fellow

drivers, who undoubtedly could guess what was occurring, was avoided, and I did my best to pretend her ass wasn't high up in the air, a banner proclaiming something of interest was taking place to any who turned their heads. The whole experience might have been more pleasurable if during the purchase of my vehicle I had not made the ill-fated choice of choosing a manual transmission.

Upon arrival at Sarah's house things quickly got more heated, especially after the prophylactics, which I always carry, put to rest the last of any doubts. It's always better to have and never need than to need and never have. For decorum's sake I will not go into details, but it's sufficient to say that the space constraints of the front seat of a Ford Focus made such movements difficult. The radio changed stations several unplanned times.

Again, perhaps all this strange behavior could be explained by me being some kind of sexual dynamo, though this seems doubtful. Another explanation may be that same as myself, she was just going with the flow. However, the cramped confines of the Focus soon had me hinting at abandoning our current place and moving it inside. She cleverly vetoed my casual suggestions by simply pretending that they never happened. Hence things continued to their natural conclusion in the tight quarters of the front passenger seat of my car.

Even given all the preceding events, this seemed rather strange. Either there was something in her house which I was not meant to see, or perhaps she had some kind of fetish involving cars. Perhaps it was an issue of trust, granted we had just met each other the day before, but such qualms seemed kind of silly given the preceding events. As well, it was not as though our coupling was a well kept secret, since the car's windows were all open and at various times during our grapple the emergency blinkers and windshield wipers mysteriously turned on, providing a nice background beat for our endeavors. It's also worth mentioning that despite the lateness of the hour at least two tired revelers happened by, including one man on a bike who made several slow passes unnoticed by my companion. In short, privacy did not seem to be an issue.

Thinking back, the car fetish theory seems more likely given that in the post-coital cool down she mentioned we'd have to do it again soon, next time parked at some high point overlooking the city. Given my age, my height, the size of my car, and my ownership of a house and bed, such an idea did not exactly fill me with lusty forward thinking thoughts. The fact that in her fervor she had seriously stretched out the neck of my favorite t-shirt did not help my feelings on the matter either.

We put back on our clothing, extracted her bike out of the back, and went our separate ways to get some sleep. I drove home, my mind filled with confusion and scrambled thoughts only broken by the discovery of a letter in my mailbox warning that my driver's license was to be restricted for earning too many points. Such points stemming from my lead foot. Knowing there was nothing to be done until morning, I laid my head upon my pillow and welcomed the silence of the night. Yes indeed, probably crazy.

Gobshite

The night air was cold. Winter was definitely on its way. Out of Leo's pocket came the metal case. He opened it and stuck a cigarillo into his mouth. The lighter flicked, once, twice, and took hold. Leo raised the golden flame towards the end of his cigarillo. The bouncer's bullet head stuck its way out the bar door.

"Hey fucker, I thought I told you to get the fuck out of here."

"Fuck you. I'm outside."

"Don't give me that shit. Get your ass off our patio."

Leo laughed and waved his arm dramatically at the two metal tables pressed up against the wall of the bar.

"Patio? You can't just throw a couple of tables and chairs on the sidewalk and call it your patio. This is a fucking public sidewalk. I'll smoke here if I want."

The bouncer opened the door all the way and took a step out. His face was red and his shoulders were rising steadily, making the man bigger. It wasn't needed. The bouncer already looked like he could take a Mack truck head on.

"I said to get the fuck out of here."

Leo knew better than to antagonize the man in his own kingdom. Lots of bulge, little brains, a bad combination. He turned and beat a hasty retreat, throwing his head back to fire off one last jibe.

"Whatever you fucking fascist."

The bouncer didn't hear. He was already ducking back into the warmth of the bar. Leo chuckled to himself again as he rounded the corner of the block. Fucking ape. Telling him what to do. What a joke. The building on the corner was dark, closed up for the night. Leo leaned up against its brick and lit his cigarillo. He inhaled and blew a smoke ring into the air. A sports car drove past. Across the street a line of twenty-somethings waited to get into a club, the girls all shivering in dresses high on sex appeal, but low on coverage. Stupid cunts. All tits and ass, no class. Leo zipped up his coat and put one hand in his pocket. Every few minutes he traded hands. The warm one for the cigarillo. The cold one into a pocket. One of the club girls bent over to adjust the strap on her high heel shoe. Leo drank in the view. Her head came up and she saw Leo staring. She gave him a dirty look. Leo laughed. Sometimes when you go fishing you don't catch what you want. The smoke from the cigarillo made its way too deep. Leo's chest heaved with a wracking cough.

"Hey, can I have one of those?"

Leo turned towards the sound of the voice. Its owner was sitting up in a sleeping bag in the entryway of the building. Dirty hands and face. Old sweatshirt full of holes. Scraggly beard. Leo ran his own hand across his whiskery face. He needed a shave. The man smiled, revealing bad teeth. Leo shrugged, partially unzipped his jacket, and pulled the metal case out of his inner coat pocket. The man leaned forward expectantly. Leo took out a cigarillo, walked over, and held it at arm's length. The man snatched it up and sniffed its length like a connoisseur. Leo closed the case and put it back into his pocket. The man's hands were shaking.

"Got a light?"

Leo took out his lighter and held it out. The man snatched it up, clumsily worked the trigger, got it going, lit his cigarillo, and handed it back. Leo put the lighter into his pocket and zipped back up his coat. It was fucking cold. The man inhaled the smoke of the cigarillo and let it out with a sigh of pleasure.

"Thank you kindly."

Leo nodded and went back to staring at the club girls across the way. They stood in huddled little groups, their faces plastered thick with makeup. They all looked very young. Dress up. Wait. Freeze to death. Get inside. Overpay for watered down drinks. Get ground on and felt up by some strange perv. Go home. Stupid bitches. Stupid life. The man in the doorway looked up at Leo, and then followed his gaze across the street.

"Checking out the knob gobblers?"

"What?"

"The girls?"

"Shut up."

The man's smile vanished.

"Excuse me?"

"I said shut up. I gave you a smoke. I don't need your commentary."

"Jesus. Just making conversation."

"Shut up."

The man's face twisted with rage and he let out a phlegmy cough.

"Fuck you ya little shit. Here's your fucking poofter cigar back."

The man threw the cigarillo at Leo. It floated halfway and dropped to the ground, orange embers rolling pitifully away. Leo laughed. The man started wrestling with his sleeping bag's zipper. Leo threw the stub of his cigarillo onto the ground, turned and walked away. As he rounded the corner he looked back. The man was picking up the stub and his own abandoned smoke. Leo laughed again. The man flipped him off.

Leo yawned. His buzz was wearing off. He was tired. It wasn't that late. There were still a lot of people out on the street. It didn't matter. He didn't know them. No reason to keep wandering around downtown in the cold all night. It would probably be best if he just walked down to the Max station and headed for home. The station was only a few blocks. A pair of happy couples passed him on the sidewalk going the other way. Each couple held themselves close together, laughing quietly at private jokes. Leo did his best not to scowl. The brunette was fairly attractive. The blonde looked like a bitch. Both of the guys looked like douchebags. Spit and polished. Brooks Brothers. Dicks. The minimart at the end of the block was still open. Light shown through the bars on the windows. Leo went inside.

A tweeker was in the back, fingering the Mountain Dews. The owner stood behind the counter, eyeing the tweeker through the convoluted system of mirrors that let him see all parts of his kingdom. The owner was of Asian descent. The tweeker was a white kid in his early twenties in need of a thorough washing. Leo walked to the back of the store, opened the cooler, and pulled out a pounder of Olympia. The tweeker watched him through the glass with bloodshot eyes.

"Watch the almonds in night time. They follow you around."

Leo glanced at the kid though the corner of his eye. "Yep."

Leo walked back to the front of the store and put the beer on the counter. The owner glanced at him, and then back up at his mirrors. He pulled out a slim paper sack and put the can of beer in it. Leo pulled two dollars out of his pocket and laid them on the counter. The owner put them in the cash register. Leo turned and left before the owner could bring back out the dime and penny that made up his change. It was still cold outside. If anything it felt colder after the warmth of the minimart. Leo cracked open the beer and took a drink. It tasted good. He took another.

The Max station platform was mostly empty. Just an old lady and a middle-aged man who looked as though he had been working late. Leo stood on the opposite end, drinking his beer and watching people walk past. With each drink he could feel his buzz building back up. Brunette hair. Pale skin beneath his fingers. Leo chugged the last quarter of the beer and threw the bag and can into the trash. A kernel of an idea. Leo chuckled to himself. A delicious idea. No. He probably shouldn't. The Max pulled up. The doors opened. People got out. People got in. Fuck it. The doors closed. The Max pulled away. Leo stood on the platform. He unzipped his coat slightly and pulled his phone and a pen from his inner pocket. He scrolled through his contacts, found the number, wrote it on his hand, put his phone back in his pocket, zipped back up his coat, and started walking. Leo smiled. This was going to be good.

Up by Kells was as good of a place as any to start. A woman and man were coming down the street the other way. Casual, but still nicely dressed. Standing apart. Talking. Both looking nervous. Not a couple, but working on it.
Perfect. Gallantry. The need to impress. Biology. Hormones. How could the man say no? Leo locked eyes and started toward them, a bounce in his step, a sloppy drunk smile on his lips. The pair stopped and eyed him with a mix of wariness and curiosity.

"Oh excuse me there, I was wondering if you could help me out?"

The Irish accent was thick to the point of being ridiculous. It didn't matter. It was all about the salesmanship. The man looked at the woman. The woman looked at the man. Both looked bemused. A hint of a smile played on the lips of the woman. The man noticed. The man took the lead.

"Uh, yeah sure, uh, what do you need?"

"Oh bless ya. I was hoping that I might be able to use your phone for just a moment."

"My phone?"

"Yes. Yes. I'm afraid I'm only visiting this fine city."

The woman piped up.

"Welcome to Portland."

An automatic response. That was good.

"Thank you lass. It's a beautiful city. However, I'm afraid me mates have gone off and moved to another pub while I was in the pisser, and now I can't find them."

The woman was smiling broadly now.

"Do you know where you're staying?"

"Somewhere out in Beaverton. That's where me mates live, but I'm afraid I don't know exactly where. If you'd just let me borrow yer phone I could give them a ring. They had me write their number on my hand just in case something like this happened."

The woman's face filled with sympathy. The man looked at Leo. The woman looked up at the man. The man sighed, dug into his pocket, and handed Leo his phone. Leo smiled and gave him a wink.

"Thank you kindly. It will only be a second."

Leo took a few steps away. The man visibly tensed up. Leo made a big show of reading the number off his hand and dialing it into the phone. He put it next to his ear. The phone rang, once, twice, three times, and connected.

"Hello?"

Leo said nothing.

"Hello? Hello? Who is this?"

Leo half-smiled and raised his eyebrows at the waiting man and woman.

"Who is this? Hello?"

The line went dead. Leo took the phone from his ear and smiled at his benefactors.

"Rang a bit and went to message. If it's okay I'd like to try one more time. You know how loud it can get in pubs.

The man nodded.

"Go right ahead."

"Sorry for the inconvenience."

"No trouble at all."

The woman grinned and sidled closer to the man. Leo made a big show of reading the number off his hand again. He put the phone to his ear. The phone rang once, twice, three times, four, five, six, seven. Voicemail. Leo hung up, walked over, and handed the phone back to the man.

"Voicemail again."

The man smiled sheepishly.

"I'm sorry man."

"Oh don't you be apologizing. Just a bit of bad luck. Nothing but a bit of cloud on a sunny day."

The man didn't seem to know what else to say. The woman was gripping onto his arm, but he looked decidedly uncomfortable.

"So, where you from?"

"Cork."

"Ireland?"

"Aye, Emerald Isle and leprechauns and all that shite."

The man smiled. The woman stared intently at Leo, her face full of concern.

"So what are you going to do?"

"Well, I'll probably just pop in and out of the different pubs around here until I find them. Noisy lot like them, they should turn up."

"Do you need any help from us?"

"Oh bless you lass, but no. You've already been more than enough help. Thank you kindly though."

The woman smiled sweetly. The man looked relieved. He started pulling the woman away.

"Well, good luck to you. Goodbye."

"Goodbye, and thank you again."

The woman turned, smiled, and waved, and then they were gone. Leo laughed quietly to himself, regained his composure, and moved off in the opposite direction. A few blocks later, down near Voodoo Donuts, he found another mark. The same speech. The same responses. A stranger handing over their phone. A number being dialed. Not once, but twice. Both times nobody picking up. Another happy couple moving off down the street with a story to tell. Leo yawned. His second buzz was wearing off. One more go, and then he'd go back to the Max station and head for home.

Back towards Kells. A young man coming out. Old style jacket over a plaid shirt. Thick frame eyeglasses. Ironic facial hair. Hipsters were almost as easy as couples. Little bastards were always thirsting for the unique, something with which to top the stories of their hipster peers. Listen to me. I met a foreign guy. He lost his friends. He borrowed my phone. He had a brogue so thick you probably could have barely understood him, but I once spent a fortnight in Dublin.

"Excuse me sir."

"Yes?"

"Would it be okay if I borrow your phone?"

"My phone?"

"Yes, it seems I've lost my friends. I'm not from here, and I'm not even sure where I'm supposed to be staying, so I need to find them again."

"Where you from?"

"Ireland."

"Welcome to Portland."

"Thank you. If I could just borrow your phone I could find out where they went."

"Of course."

The hipster handed over his phone. Leo took a few steps away. The hipster watched with interest, likely already rehearsing how he would tell the story. Leo dialed the number into the phone. It rang once, twice, thrice, and connected.

"Hello?"

Leo half-smiled at the hipster.

"Hello? Who is this?"

Leo shrugged his shoulders. Miming that he was getting sent to voicemail.

"Leo? Is this you? You fucking tiny dick bastard."

Leo's fingers tightened around the phone. The smile fell from his lips. His brow furrowed. The hipster started looking concerned. The last of Leo's buzz drained away.

"Cunt."

"Jesus fucking Christ Leo. Really? You're using other people's phones now? What the fuck is wrong with you? It's been three fucking months. You have to let this go."

"Three years of my life bitch."

The hipster's eyes were round in his face. He started to move forward. Leo spun around. The voice in his ear beat into his head.

"Go get yourself some god damn help. I swear if you keep this shit up I'm going to call the cops, you fucking psycho."

Leo swung the phone in front of his mouth and screamed at the top of his lungs.

"Cunt!"

The voice on the other end yelled back, but he couldn't hear it. The hipster snatched the phone away and hit disconnect. Tears flowed down Leo's face. Other pedestrians stopped and stared. The hipster, beat red, starting screaming at Leo.

"What the fuck man?! What the fuck?!"

Leo's fist connected with the hipster's nose. The hipster went down, sprawled out on the sidewalk. Leo ran away as fast as he could. After about ten blocks, and several corners, he slowed to a walk. The block was empty. Fuck. What the fuck? Tears still flowed down his cheeks. He snorted and spit a loogey onto the sidewalk. Bitch. Just a fucking bitch. Three years. Three fucking years. Leo wiped his eyes, smearing the phone number written on the back of his hand into an unintelligible mess.

Protest

Evening time. Downtown. Keller Fountain Park.
Monument to an autocrat long dead. Artificial cliffs of concrete.
Gurgling waterfalls run empty. Cement islands in a dry sea. In
summer time it would be alive. Pools shaded from the heat of
the sun by mighty boughs. It's winter now. The water is gone.
The trees stand over all with skeletal limbs outstretched at the
rising masses of steel and glass which climb upwards on all sides
towards the sky. It's quiet now. Too cold to be wandering about
without reason. Now is the time to sit cozy watching Netflix.
It's Thursday. Tomorrow is a work day. Maybe everyone will
try harder when the weekend comes.

The running group comes in spurts. Shotgun blasts of
indeterminate size and force. Small groups of twos and threes
with the occasional lone wolf prowling through the expanse.
The light at the crosswalk turns and some are held back. The
rest come forward, across the top of the cliffs, and down the
stairs, hopping from island to island despite the lack of worry
over wet shoes and socks. They yell in their excitement as they

come, trampling traces of flour laid prior to show them the way. One finds the bag of beer at the base of one of the silent waterfalls, hidden away in the shadows, safe from roving teenagers and hobos. With a cheer he hoists it up to the others, and they rip open the black plastic to joyfully consume the contents held within.

Paul comes in by himself. After the quickest of the runners, but before the start of the walkers. A small dog on a leash runs next to him. It's not his dog. It belongs to a friend. A favor. The dog is quick, but getting tired. Paul is tired too, but the dog is an easier excuse to swallow. It's good to run the dog. Running the dog makes it tired. A tired dog will sleep most of the night. Paul jumps from island to island, coaxing the dog to follow, waiting for the little creature to get up the nerve for each jump. The men and women of the running group greet him with jeers and a cold can of cheap beer. Paul opens the can and takes a slug. The sweat dries beneath his clothes, a cool layer beneath the insulation.

The walkers come in. Probably around fifteen or so runners and walkers all together. They divide into knots of conversation, covering the various factions of life. Paul moves from group to group, avoiding any talks that seem too serious. He doesn't stay with one group for long. He isn't thirsty for conversation, at least not of the two way variety. He is mostly just happy to listen tonight. He's been sick most of the week. Under the weather. The less exertion the better. The beer probably won't help, but fuck it, not everything is supposed to help. He wanders around and looks into nooks and crannies. Dead leaves and other remains. One secluded corner is filled with an impressive amount of empty plastic slurpee cups. Somebody is a person of habit.

They are there for maybe a little over twenty minutes. Somebody yells and the last dregs are emptied from cans, some down throats and some onto concrete. A few of the men take pisses in corners. A few of the women roll their eyes, though more than one has wished for a similar convenience. The ripped plastic bag is wadded up and thrown into the garbage. The empty cans are stacked around the top edge, easier to collect for anyone more desperate for the nickels. Karl, the big man, leaves one unopened beer with the empties, a special treat for the first to find the treasure.

The tribe regathers and pull themselves up and out of the dry sea. The little dog is less careful with its leaps, more confident now that's it's done it a couple of times. All the leaps are well timed. Not a single incident. They move to the corner of Third and Clay where an X is marked in flour. Which way? This way? Did anyone see which way they went? The runners go silent. There's noise in the distance. Another group approaches, larger and louder, voices in a rhythmic beat of disdain. Runner's ears try to divide off distraction, try to discern meaning from the noise.

"No justice. No peace. No justice. No peace. No justice. No peace."

They come up Third, large knots steadily marching down the middle of the street. Some carry signs and other umbrellas. Even the righteous need to be protected from the rain. The protest must be somewhere around two hundred people. They shout in unison up and down the line. The mouths of some are covered by bandanas, a few decorated by maniacal skeletal grins. Some leave their faces naked to the world, unafraid of who sees what they do. There are a few old ones, but most are young, early twenties or younger. Pretty much all of them are white, though to be fair, in this city, it's not so common to be anything else.

The runners stand on their corner, safe on the sidewalk from the approaching flood. The marchers turn from Third and start making their way up Clay, moving past with a steady beat of mouth and feet. A white minivan comes up and stops at the intersection. The driver seems unsure. Portions of the back half of the mass begin to split off. Ten or so, but not more. Those with covered faces and dark clothes. Others slow or stop, turning to watch. A few hold phones up above their heads, glass eyes watching everything, electronic ears recording narrations of the scene.

The rebel mass groups around the minivan. The driver hits his turn signal for a left, looking to get away, but it's too late. They enwrap the front half of the vehicle. They shout and chant. They wave their arms victoriously in the air, these conquerors of the Honda Odyssey. The minivan tries to inch its way forward. Some of the group fall back, but others rush in to take their place. Hands press up against metal and glass. The minivan tries to inch its way forward again. One of the would be conquerors throws himself to the ground. A new chant erupts from several corners, less unified in beat, but not in purpose.

"We're recording. We're recording."

"Fucking protesters. What a bunch of bullshit."

The old runner next to Paul says it loud. Paul wishes he would have said it quieter. The loud sound of an umbrella smacking the side of the minivan echoes off a building, followed by an animalistic groan of half disapproval and half approval from the crowd.

"God damn it."

Karl breaks away from the runners and starts making his way across the street. Karl is a large man. A shaved bear of a man, but bigger. Every step is light like a dancer's, but heavy with the mass it carries. A thick red beard covers his face. The start of a beer belly only adds to the grandeur. Karl is built like a brick shit house. A few other runners follow him across the street, planets orbiting a sun. Karl towers over the kids around the minivan. He pushes his way through the outskirts until he's in amongst them. He moves through them with the gentle hand of a farmer making his way through his wheat field. He stops near the crowd, arms crossed on his chest, and glares. He does not raise his voice when he speaks. Teenage eyes make their way up and down. The less brave begin to break away. One of the retreating youth sidles his way near to Paul. He has wild eyes, pumped full of adrenaline.

"The guy in the van said he had a glock man."

The youth moves away up the street. A woman, slightly older, makes her way over. The youth has designated Paul as the leader. The woman's around twenty-five. Long brown frizzy hair frames her face. She's attractive, about a seven, maybe an eight if she cleaned herself up a bit. Paul feels weird making such a mental note. It doesn't seem appropriate for the time, but there it is. Automatic. To mate or not to mate. Does this one meet the lizard brain's criteria? It's not logical. There's nothing one can do but ignore it and use the parts of the mind that make us human. She stops in front of Paul and gestures towards the minivan.

"Did you see what happened?"

Paul doesn't really want to answer. He doesn't want to get involved, but finally he acquiesces.

"I saw a bunch of people blocking a minivan."

"These people are protesting the police shooting their friend. A seventeen year old kid."

These people? Was she not one of them herself? Was she not protesting? Just tagging along to provide free explanation to any passerby?

"A police officer shot him and nothing is being done."

Gears click their way forward in Paul's mind. Seventeen year old kid. A black kid. Shot about a week ago. He wasn't up on all the details. Police claimed he was a robbery suspect. Ran away from the cops. Had a replica gun. A tragedy. Friends and family say he was a good kid, a sweet boy. Boiled down you get either gun happy cops shoot kid or kid does something stupid and gets shot. Two completely opposite dinners from the same ingredients. Just add a little heat. Paul doesn't know. The devil's in the details. He doesn't know the details. People don't care about the details. People prefer their stories boiled down. They're easier to digest.

"What's that have to do with the van?"

The woman is getting frustrated. She looks more attractive when she's mad. Stupid lizard brain. The little dog pulls on its leash. It's getting nervous. It doesn't take a lot to make most little dogs get nervous. Probably afraid of getting stepped on.

"That vehicle hit one of our group and nearly ran him over. We'd be very appreciative if you would tell the police what you saw."

Paul looks the woman in the eye. There's no signs of untruth. Nothing to give her away. She's adamant. Forceful. An all in defender of the world her words have weaved.

"I don't want to get involved."

The woman looks disappointed. She takes a deep breath. She's not done yet. A cry goes up from someone further up the street.

"C'mon, keep moving forward. C'mon, let's go."

The crowd around the van disperses and begins moving up Clay at a trot. The watchers turn as well, though some hang back. The back end of the mass breaks away, moving to catch up with their fellows that have continued moving on ahead. The minivan turns and makes its escape, up the street a block and parks. Police on bicycles come up Clay, they take up position blocking the street. A white van moves in behind them, police in riot gear hanging off the outside. Turtle men and women with faces hidden behind plastic visors. The last of the watchers turn and move away. One of the bike cops break off to talk with the minivan, and the rest move up the street. The running group on the sidewalk watch them pass. Karl and his pilot fish rejoin the main group. One of their fellows on the sidewalk pipes up with a question.

"What did the driver look like?"

Karl half rolls his eyes and answers, his voice dripping with sarcasm.

"He was wearing a bright red 'Make America Great Again' hat.

A pause. Everyone stares at Karl. The big man spits and starts again, impatience in his tone.

What do you think? He looked like a scared old man trying to get home."

The running group shuffles its feet. A few quietly move away to find the right direction. The scouts begin shouting out their finds. True trail is found. A couple people crack jokes about what they saw. Someone calls the big man Charles Atlas. He laughs good naturedly. Maybe next time he can rip off his shirt to show off his leopard leotard and start working out with some large triangular weights. The group laughs. The herd begins to move en masse, off in the opposite direction of the confusion.

When Is It Due

Katie announced her pregnancy at the barbeque. The women made their sounds of delight, sweeping in to hug their friend. The men smiled and shook Kevin's hand, voicing their congratulations and trading a few jokes as they always did when they were unsure what to say. Katie beamed, a sleek porpoise riding the waves of attention and affection now flowing her way. Kevin blushed and smiled big, a nervous bit player in the upcoming production. Of the friends, Devin was the loudest. She squealed and babbled, her voice rising in volume, her eyes getting watery. She jumped up and down in her excitement, holding Katie's hands in her own. Devin's boyfriend, Leo, was out on the balcony, grilling burgers. He did not come inside to see about the commotion emanating from the open glass door. He stared down at the sizzling meat and grease fueled flames as though nothing else in the world mattered.

Lisa did her part. She went and gave Katie a hug and voiced the proper words. Then she moved back and watched the commotion from the perimeter. She was unsure how to hold her hands. Pockets seemed too casual, arms crossed too stand-offish, and clasped in front far too formal. One of Lisa's hands unconsciously tucked a blonde lock of hair behind her ear. Devin had her hands up, clutched as though in prayer. She went outside and yelled the news to Leo, who only grunted his affirmation of having heard. All conversations in the room were derailed, forced onto a new single track. When is it due? How long have you known? Do you know what it is? The carrier was coy, basking in her moment. Lisa's eyes tracked across the room, studying pictures and random art purchased at yard sales and Goodwill. Her stomach gurgled, an uncomfortable shift in its arrangement.

Lisa moved to the kitchen and poured herself a glass of wine. She sipped slowly. The sounds of the living room were subdued but still noticeable. Buns, lettuce, tomatoes, and sliced cheese waiting in neat piles for the burgers to be done. Potato and macaroni salad sat in their containers, the plastic film on top still intact. Everything ready. Everything waiting. Devin came in, a too wide grin stretching its way across her face, tears flowing down her cheeks. She dabbed her face with a dish towel, poured herself a glass of wine, and downed half of it with a single gulp.

"I can't believe it. It's just so exciting, isn't it?"

Lisa forced a smile.

"Yes, very exciting."

Devin took another drink of wine and wiped her eyes again.

"I'm just so happy for them."

Devin chattered on. Katie would make such a great mother. Kevin would be such a good father. They'd be the best parents. She had known it would just be a matter of time. They were so lucky. Auntie Devin would spoil the shit out of that kid. Lisa nodded, but her eyes kept skipping away, taking in every detail of the small kitchen. The twist in her gut was growing. She was feeling a little sick.

"There's no watermelon."

Devin was startled from her soliloquy.

"What?"

"No one brought a watermelon. You can't have a barbeque without a watermelon."

Devin bent her head to the side in puzzlement, the teeth of her grin stained red by the wine.

"I'm sure nobody cares."

"Nonsense. I'll just pop out to the store and grab one."

Lisa put down her wine glass and moved back into the living room. Devin followed, but split off to rejoin the celebratory group. Lisa slipped out the door, through the hall, down the stairs, and into the sunshine of the outside world. Devin was out on the balcony, having a quiet argument with Leo. Lisa moved on without listening. The apartment building was a four story structure of weathered brick and old time charm. Lisa wondered if Kevin and Katie would retain their current domicile, or migrate. It didn't matter really. They would do what they did. Change was inevitable.

It was a half mile walk to the Safeway. The streets were crowded, but they felt less stifling than inside the apartment. Lisa's stomach had unclenched the moment she walked out the door. Summer was coming to an end. The air was crisp and flavored by scents of decay. Tourists and locals shuffled through the hemmed in streets of downtown. An aimless herd on the move, dodging each other, banging into one another, and only stopping when commanded to by the stern red hand of the crosswalk light. Katie pregnant. How about that? They'd known each other since college. Katie had been the Maid of Honor at her wedding, and the one to take her out drinking during the divorce. Crazy Katie. It seemed strange. A different person. Paul had always wanted kids. At least he had always said he did. Lisa had never really been all that sure. She wasn't against the idea, but it really wasn't a demanding urge either.

When Lisa was in nursing school she had worked in the maternity ward. It hadn't been what she wanted to specialize in, but they all had to. It was one thing to read about it in text books. It was another to see it in person. The screaming. The stretching. The tearing. The shit. The literal fucking shit. It had been disgusting. However, when all was said and done, not one had ever looked disappointed. They had all looked so serene. Thirty-five. It wasn't really all so uncommon now. Even forty was not outside the norm. Life was not so bad now. Why transform it? Just musings. A lot of steps would have to be done before that one. A lot of choices. Paul would make a good father, but that was no longer her concern. Did he still want kids? When he looked at his black haired mouse, did he ever picture a squirming bundle in her arms?

The last bit of the walk was diagonal across the park. The red and white sign of the grocery store was visible across from the far corner. The homeless sat on the benches and watched the luckier ones move past. The sidewalk was less crowded. The bums made the tourists nervous, only the locals moved through the gauntlet. The bums stood alone and in clusters. Smoking cigarettes. Asking for change. Eyeing the world through glazed eyes. Some talking to others. Some talking to no one in particular. One man was yelling at the statue of Lincoln in the park center. All had been babies once.

What was it like to carry a baby? It seemed strange. Almost like having a parasite. The thought made Lisa feel sick. Something alive, growing inside, a part of you, but independent. Paul's mother had once said that having a baby was just getting a dog that learned how to talk and tell people your secrets. That didn't sound right, but maybe for Paul it had been, he was a bit labradorish in character. Life. There was life in Katie's belly. A belly that had been used repeatedly for body shots while in Cancun. That had been a long a time ago. Crazy Katie having a baby, and looking as tranquil as Lisa had ever seen her.

The inside of the store was almost too cold. They had the air conditioning up and running. Lisa went back to the produce and found the watermelons in their high cardboard box on the floor. She selected a seedless one, perfectly round, smooth green skin, probably five pounds in weight. She hefted it and moved to the front of the store. She read the covers of the celebrity rags while she waited in line at the checkout counter. She moved to the front of the line. The woman at the register was in her early sixties. Lined face, thinning hair, and a gap between her two front teeth. She rang up the watermelon with a slow but steady hand. Five and a half pounds. Lisa had been close.

"Having a barbeque?"

"Yeah."

"It's the weather for it. You wanna bag?"

"No thank you."

Lisa paid for the watermelon and headed for the automatic doors. The glass slid open. A woman ponderously made her way inside. She was younger than Lisa, probably in her late twenties. She was around seven months pregnant, her belly large and round, her body thrown back to account for the extra mass. Lisa moved out of the way as the woman waddled into the store. She glowed. All eyes were upon her. The feelings of goodwill radiating through the air towards her from her adoring spectators was palpable. The woman smiled her thanks as she moved past. Lisa carried her watermelon outside.

What was it like? What was it like to be that woman? To look so uncomfortable, but yet so sedate. A misshapen goddess adored by all. An ideal form beaten into ruin by the ravages of motherhood. The park was nearly empty. Just the homeless, milling about, filling space. What did it feel like to have that growing weight? It couldn't be easy. A wild thought flit through Lisa's brain. She held the watermelon, running her fingers across its shining rind. She was wearing a loose sweater. She slipped the watermelon under her sweater, and clasped her hands beneath to support it. The round mass pressed against her stomach. It was cold. One of the hobos cackled. He was watching her, itching his chin through a greasy beard. Lisa ignored him and moved on.

It didn't seem so bad. At the edge of the park she waited for the signal, and then crossed into the thick mass of pedestrians. It was different. No one bumped into her. Nobody jostled her. Everyone was careful to give her extra space. The crowds parted. Eyes fell to her falsified belly and gentle smiles crossed downturned lips. Strangers bowed their heads in greeting. Old and young alike beamed with happiness. Couples took each other's hands and gave each other a gentle squeeze. Old women gave her knowing looks, remembering their own time in the sun. Children openly stared, their mouths agape. She was an island. Heathen and saint alike bowed to the power within her belly. The power of new life. A last bit of magic in a world with little to none. Lisa felt her steps become slow and easy. She floated on an altruistic sea created by those around her.

Lisa's arms were getting tired and sore. The red hand flashed and the crowd came to a halt to wait. Across the street, at the front of the mass, stood a woman, the belly beneath her shirt equal in size with the fraudulent mass beneath Lisa's. Their eyes met. The woman smiled with understanding. They were companions. Equals. Sisters. Two divine beings afoot amongst the mortals. Lisa smiled back.

A man next to Lisa reached over to stroke the watermelon beneath her sweater. Lisa jerked away, her hands instinctively moving to stop his unwanted advance. The watermelon dropped to the ground. It shattered on the sidewalk with a wet splat. Red mush speckled the concrete and the legs of the waiting people. Eyes were wide in faces contorted with shock. Somebody gasped. Across the street, the other woman's face went from confusion to disgust. The bond was gone. Lisa was nothing. A liar. A false idol. A man began to laugh. The signal changed.

The woman started to cross the street, her eyes locked on the phony before her. Lisa turned and fled.

Gutterball

He stands six lanes down. He's not a friend, just an
acquaintance, someone whose existence you acknowledge, but
little else. You are in the same running group, but you've barely
ever spoken. You can see him across the gleaming refracted
light of spinning balls, racing their way frantically down the
oiled wood. He's a big man, not tall, but wide. Big shoulders,
big chest, and big arms, stretching his black t-shirt so tight that it
looks to be several sizes too small. He's starting to get fat, not
overly so, just the beginning signs. The type of chunkiness
gained by former weight lifters. The added bulk of a man who
used to pump iron at the gym every day, but has since given it up
for whatever reason. Just the starting signs. The gradual bulging
of the gut. The slow collapse of the pectorals. A physical
specimen slowly but surely collapsing from the peak of his
perceived former glory. The steady ruination of an oversized
monolith due to the lack of maintenance.

You wish she had never told you.

"Can I talk to you about something?"

"Sure, what's up?"

He's bowling. His lumbering size is strangely graceful.
Each step floating his mass across the floor. His stair step calves
tighten. His body lowers. His arm, the upper half covered in
tattoos, whips back and extends. The ball in his meaty hand,
covered in green swirls, softly kisses the hardwood without a
sound. The holes slip from his fingers. The growing thunder of
the roll, right down the center, building to a cataclysmic rumble
as the ball strikes the pins. They fall as one and he raises his
arms in triumph, turning back to his spectators at the lane who
greet his feat with howls of victory.

You sit with your friend. The tears in her eyes the only sign
of emotion. A story told in a voice that is flat and monotone.

His spectators are made up of a woman and a little girl. The
girl can't be much more than five. You had heard that he had a
daughter. Somebody had told you, a fact in passing, or perhaps
it had just been something you had once overheard. Now living
proof stands in front of you. Big brown eyes and dark brown
hair. She has her father's nose and mouth. The rest must come
from her mother. Who knows? You have never met the woman.
A phantom from a past life. Briefly mentioned like the daughter,
a fact without further explanation. An ex long gone before you
ever met him.

"What do you want me to do?"

"Nothing."

The little girl is wearing a pink shirt, emblazoned with Hello
Kitty, and black tights. She's jumping with excitement. Little
red lights built into the heels of her princess covered sneakers
flash every time her feet touch the ground. Her hair, in a
ponytail, whips up and down. There's a hole in her tights. A
small one on the left knee. White skin pale against the black.
The smile on her face is his smile. The same toothy grin. The
same gap between the upper two front teeth.

You can hear her voice in your head. You can see the words emerge from her lips, each one part of a steady dirge, pounding with the resonating regularity of a clock tower at midnight. The words come out, but she has gone away.

"It was a long time ago. Over a year."

The woman with him is a stranger. She is short and a little round, just enough to make everything pop in the right places. She is a little too done up for your taste. Dyed jet black hair hangs loose to her shoulders. Skin tanned much darker than the current natural sources of light had any hope of producing. She wears tight black jeans, a fashionable white loose fitting top, and multiple gaudy bracelets on both her wrists. Too much makeup. Dark eye shadow. Thick mascara. She looks out of place amongst the aging decor, cracked vinyl seats, and stained ceiling tiles of the bowling alley. He sits down and takes a sip from a glass of beer on the table. She gets up and bends over to pick up her ball. He says something you cannot hear. She rises and turns back to look at him and replies, a coy gaze targeted his way. A little smile, narrowed eyes, and cocked hip speak more than words. He laughs and she laughs too. The little girl sits and sips her soda, oblivious to the interplay between the two adults. Unaware of a world that will only reveal itself with time, the opening of a treasure chest full of cursed gold.

"Don't tell anybody."

"Okay. I promise."

You wish she had never told you. Why did she have to tell you? She is a friend, but not a close friend. Why did she have to force you into a limbo with no way out? A world of knowledge without action. A co-conspirator in a secret that's not yours, but has somehow become yours to keep. You feel guilty for such thoughts, but they sit there in the back, furiously raising their hands, desperately trying to call attention to themselves. Of course she had to tell someone. Of course she had to share. She's your friend. It's what friends are for, but still, still you can't deny that part of you wishes she had told someone else. Part of you feels dejection at the added weight of the load placed upon your back. You were glad to be there for her. You were glad she had someone she could trust. The weight is nothing compared to what she herself must have to carry. The description nothing compared to the actual experience. It's not even close.

"I was asleep. We'd both been drinking. I didn't want him to drive home. I woke up to him inside me."

You sit and stare at him as he sips his beer. You sit and stare at this acquaintance of yours, a man you have known for several years, but don't really know beyond the few passing facts. You sit and you stare at him, trying to hate, trying to feel disdain. He is nothing to you, just above being another anonymous face in the crowd. The few facts you know only due to the coincidence of group dynamics. Two people. Same place, same time. He is not your friend. You've never done anything but exchange pleasantries, follow the social norms, and now it is required that you hate him. Hate him for what he has done. Hate him for committing such a cardinal sin.

"You should do something."

"I don't want to."

He looks up and notices you across the way. Your eyes lock across the distance. He gives you a little nod and raises his hand in greeting. The reaction is automatic. Your hand raises back, a mirrored gesture. You lower your hand and look away. Your hand feels dirty. You stifle the rising need to go into the bathroom and wash it. He looks confused for a moment then looks away, his shoulders shrugging. The connection is too small for your strange reaction to spark much thought or worry. The bastard. The fucking bastard. He sits there in the gleaming fluorescent light. Relaxed. Happy. Enjoying the undeserved bounty of his time. You want to stand up. You want to point your finger. You want to denounce him. Declare to the world what he is. What he has done.

"Don't tell anybody. Do nothing. It was such a long time ago. Nearly a year."

It's the little girls turn to bowl. He stands up and pulls over a metal stand, a sloping ramp of stiff wires which goes from waist height down to the floor. The little girl watches with eyes wide open, taking everything in. He lifts up a ball with purple swirls and places it on the top. He lets the little girl instruct him how to aim it, pushing the bottom end with a few well placed taps of his foot. The little girl makes loud demands, contradicting the last command. He dutifully follows each order, eyes twinkling, mirth playing across his lips. The woman watches from her seat, sitting back, sipping on a beer. Her face gives away the emotions of her mind. Warmth. Adoration. The planting of the seeds of love.

"This is hard for me to say, but I need to say it to somebody I need to tell somebody."

Nothing. There is nothing you can do. You have made a promise. Given your word. It is not your place. Not your sin. You are not the victim. You do not get to decide. Rapist. He is a rapist. You yearn to say the words. To fall upon him with righteous indignation. To shatter the facade and reveal to all the ugliness underneath. To unmask the monster that lies within. To watch the adoring eyes of the woman with him turn to disgust and horror. Sucked in. You've been sucked into a vortex. She is not a close friend, but she is a friend. A promise is a promise. The bastard. The fucking bastard.

"You're an easy person to talk to. I feel like you're somebody I can trust. Is it okay if I tell you something?"

The anger subsides and falls back. You dig deeper, trying to restart the flow, but the well has run dry. There is no way to sustain it. You are not the victim. You are none of these people. Truth be told both he and the one you call your friend could drift

out of your life and leave no mark. It is a terrible thought to
have. One tinged by further pangs of guilt, but there it is. You
don't want to see her hurt, but there is nothing you can do after
the fact. Just sit with the knowledge you've been told not to
share by the very person on whose behalf you feel the need to try
and fill yourself with rage. Without sufficient emotion such
passion is unsustainable.

"I see him around sometimes. It doesn't bother me much
anymore. What's done is done."

What are you supposed to do? You are neither judge nor
jury. You are just someone who was there to listen when
someone needed to talk. A proxy by happenstance. Now
obligated to feel the anger required by society. Forced to take up
the mantle of the right against the wrong. What was described to
you wasn't right, what was described to you wasn't fair, but you
weren't there. You don't know. Does he even know? Does he
even know the harm that he has caused? The hurt that he has
wrought? If you were to march over and tell him that you know,
would you be met with denials, or would you be met with horror
and tears? Would he be a monster, or a man scared of himself,
desperately wishing he could be washed clean of his sins? Your
promise has left you neutered. You will never know. You can
never ask. All you can do is stare and wonder. All you can do is
keep your mouth shut and hope. Hope that he is a man and not a
monster. Hope that the terror he fashioned was a mistake and
not a trend. You don't know. There is no way for you to know.

"Have you ever said anything to him?"

"No."

He helps the little girl push the ball down the ramp. It picks
up speed and she squeals in delight. He crouches beside her,
watching the progress of their efforts. The woman in the seat
leans forward. Watching. Waiting. The ball slowly glides to
the left. Inch by steady inch. It grazes the furthest pin as it rolls
past. The pin shakes. The pin shudders. The pin falls. The

little girl screams with joy. The woman hoots and claps her hands. He stands and tosses the little girl into the air. He lifts her onto his broad shoulder. The little girl is smiling, one fist pumping the air, the other holding tight to her daddy who parades her about, celebrating her victory.

"What do you want me to do?"

"Nothing."

You feel a nudge on your side. It's your turn again to bowl. You return to the broader world. You rise and pick up your ball. It's green with swirls. It feels heavy in your hands. You insert your fingers into the holes. Your steps move you forward. Your arm extends back. Your arm arcs forward. You can see them from the corner of your eye. All three are smiling. All three are happy.

"Can I talk to you about something?"

The ball clatters into the lane, a resounding thud that draws in eyes from all around. The ball slides down the lane, straight into the gutter. Everyone but you looks away.

"Don't tell anybody."

Dancer

With a deft motion of your hand she spins and a smile spreads across her face. You let a smile spread across your own in return. She twirls and you twirl after her, sweat forming on your forehead. Both of your heads kick back and let the centrifugal force take hold. She laughs, with her raven hair spilling out in an undulating wave behind her. Your hands, your wrists, your arms, your body, and your feet. All are instruments playing in concert to create something beautiful. Her body slides against yours and she lets you conduct the way forward. She is no slouch herself, and the dual concerts of your forms play in harmony, matching movement by movement.

"Trust me."

Your voice is low, but firm. You bring her into your arms and throw her backwards towards the ground. A gasp, a tightening of muscles, nervous laughter turns to joy as her fall is stopped short, she is left to hang, and then brought back from the depths. This is your moment. The instance where you can do no wrong. While the music plays you are the center of the world, a potential finally reached, a sparrow no more.

The sparrow is a nervous little bird. It hops from tree to tree, chirping little quips before moving on again. The sparrow hides from the world. The sparrow is not brave or bold, but out here while the music plays, you are not a sparrow. Out here while the music plays, you are everything. The whole world has stopped to watch. Men wish they were you and women wish they were in your arms. You are the peacock, the most beautiful of all the birds, and your plumage is spread wide for all the world to see.

The peacock is a haughty bird, overly proud and so very vain. But still the peacock has its fears, and often runs away. You are not the peacock, more like an eagle or bird of prey. Out on the floor you dance. No doubts, no worries, no niggling little voices whispering that you look a fool. There is no little outside camera view that reveals all of your mistakes. No, as long as the music plays there is none of this. You exude great confidence with every motion and every word you say. You're not boasting and you're not hoping, it's a universal truth. Out here with her in your arms you are more than you've ever been. Each dip, each twirl, each spin, she leans back in your arms to swoon. You don't even know her name, and she has no idea of yours, but it doesn't matter. At this moment you are everything and more.

The music stops and the dance ends. She says her thanks which you politely give back in kind. You know nothing of this girl, and she knows nothing about you. You look into her eyes, and she looks back before you look away. You try to start a question, but it dies before it even begins. You separate and she moves off, back to her other suitors and her friends. You want to step forward. You want to at least ask her for her name, but you make excuses and you silently walk away. You have become the sparrow once again.

How Was Montana

The two crossfitters stood in the middle of the park. The woman had blonde hair drawn up in a ponytail. The man had thick black hair and a beard. The woman wore tight spandex and a sports bra. The man wore basketball shorts and a black tank top. The woman was small, but fit. Toned muscles. Flat belly. The man was big. Not fat, just big. He probably outweighed the woman by a good seventy pounds. He had a barrel chest and a thick middle. He stood perfectly straight, his back braced, his large legs rooted to the ground. The woman hung off of him, her thighs pressed into his armpits, her knees and calves gripping tightly. His hands supported her ass. Her arms crossed over her chest, she laid back, pulled herself up, and laid back again. Each sit up carried her through a 180 degree arc. Every muscle in her stomach and back stood out. Twenty, twenty-five, thirty reps. The woman stopped, the man's beard tickling her where the bottom of her sports bra met bare skin. The man started doing squats.

Phoebe watched from the cafe table across the street. Her fingers brushed a strand of hair behind her ear, pausing for a moment to squeeze her earlobe between her index and middle finger, her pinky at the corner of her mouth. The hand migrated down her neck, around her breast, and onto her belly. She self-consciously pulled the hem of her shirt lower. Two forgotten cups of coffee sat on the table. Forgotten. Devin stared at the blanket wrapped baby in her arms. Her smiling mouth made cooing sounds. Her index finger was wrapped tightly in a little fist. The baby looked at Devin, then at the clouds floating by overhead, then at Devin again.

"Is he doing much smiling yet?"

Phoebe's gaze broke away from the crossfitters. She looked across the table at the baby in Devin's arms.

"Huh?"

"I said is he doing much smiling yet?"

"Yeah, he's smiling quite a bit anymore. When the mood strikes him."

The baby kicked his legs, throwing off the confining layers of the blanket. Devin giggled and tucked the blanket back around and under.

"He is just so damn cute."

"Yeah, he's really something."

"I'm just so jealous."

Phoebe glanced back at the crossfitters. The woman was doing sit ups again. For a moment, at the pause at the bottom of the down swing, their eyes met. Phoebe averted her gaze. She studied the cars parked along the street. Her hand pulled self-consciously at the bottom of her shirt again.

"Thanks again for meeting up. It's been too long since I've been out of the house."

Devin didn't look up. All her focus was on the squirming pink mass in her arms.

"I'm always free to see this little bundle of joy."

Phoebe picked up her coffee mug and took a sip. She made a face and put it back down. The coffee had gone cold. Her hand rested on the mug, toying with its handle. Devin murmured baby talk at the baby, tickling his belly, trying to get him to smile. Phoebe breathed in deep, and let it out. Her fingers drummed the table. She lightly bit her lower lip.

"So how was Montana?"

Devin did not look up.

"Montana was good. The usual."

"Do anything fun?"

"Went fishing with my brother. Leo just stayed at the house and drank beer with my dad the whole time. I swear the two hardly left the living room."

"I didn't know your dad and Leo got along that well."

"Not really. There he goes."

The baby smiled and kicked his legs. Devin giggled, her face split by a joyous grin.

"Who's a happy little man? Huh? Who's a happy little man?"

Phoebe turned back towards the park. The crossfit couple were gone. Probably jogging, or maybe calling it a day to get a beer. A minivan drove by. The driver, a woman, a look of harried desperation in her eye, hunched forward over the steering wheel. Two bouncing kids sat in the back. The sun peaked through the clouds. It felt good on Phoebe's skin.

"You and Leo ever going to have one?"

Devin looked up at Phoebe, her smile gone.

"Doubt it. I can't even get the fucker to ask me to marry him."

Devin looked back down at the baby and her smile returned.

"I wish the jackass would hurry up already. You know, the clock is ticking."

Phoebe tried to smile, but was only half successful. Devin didn't notice. The baby was smiling again. A breeze blew through the trees along the street and in the park. The branches swayed and the leaves danced. Phoebe looked down at her coffee cup and rubbed her temples with her thumb and index finger. Devin rocked the baby in her arms.

"How's Nick been doing?"

Phoebe looked up at Devin, then over her shoulder at a couple walking down the street holding hands.

"He's good. He's been having to work a lot. I think he's been pretty beat."

"I bet Nick is a good dad."

The couple smiled at each other. The man leaned in for a quick kiss.

"Yeah, he is. I've been pumping and he handles the feeding every other night. Nick just adores the shit out of him."

The baby arched his back and let out a screech. His little face squelched up and he began to cry, flapping his chubby little arms. Phoebe reached forward, her face etched with concern.

"You want me to take him?"

Devin pulled away.

"No. No. It's okay."

Devin started gently bouncing the baby, softly cooing and clicking her tongue. The baby kept crying, his face turning red. Two old men at the next table looked over, one face cross, the other lifted by a gentle sentimental smile. Phoebe wagged her fingers.

"C'mon, hand him over. He's probably getting tired or hungry."

Devin ignored Phoebe. Her bouncing shifted to rocking, and the soft cooing continued. The baby let out one or two more fitful cries, gave a big yawn, and fell asleep. Devin smiled and giggled.

"There you go. There you go tired little man. Just sleepy. That's all."

Phoebe leaned back in her chair. The old man with the sentimental smile gave her a wink before rejoining his cantankerous table mate in conversation. Devin looked up at Phoebe, still smiling, but her eyes sad.

"You are just so lucky."

A songbird landed on the hood of a red BMW parked across the street. The bird shook out its feathers, tweeted a few precursory notes, and took a shit on the gleaming metal surface. Phoebe breathed in, and audibly let it out.

"You think Leo wants to have kids?"

One side of Devin's face curled downwards. Her eyes met Phoebe's, fell back to the baby, and then drifted off down the street.

"I think the bastard secretly got a vasectomy."

"What makes you say that?"

"I quit taking the pill a year ago."

The bird flew away. Phoebe watched it glide across the park, gaining altitude with each flap. Devin leaned forward, her face serious.

"Don't tell Leo."

Phoebe swallowed and licked her lips. They felt dry. Cracked.

"Which part?"

"Just don't tell him."

Devin's eyes bored into Phoebe's. Phoebe looked back out across the park, hoping to see the bird, but it was gone. The baby gurgled. He was awake again. Devin leaned back and made kissy sounds at him. Phoebe watched, staring at the bundle in Devin's arms. She unconsciously took another drink of her coffee and grimaced. Still cold. She put the mug down.

"So how's your family in Montana doing?"

Bogey At Ten O'Clock

Goldrush, an annual hash campout. A hundred and fifty weirdos and freaks packed into a private campground on the coast. An excuse to get away from reality for an extended period. A chance to be entirely yourself, to not worry about what the wider world would think of your behavior. Whatever you are, let it all hang out. The Goldrush weekend is the epitomy of what hashing is all about.

She's nervous. She smiles at me but then looks away, blushing. Everyone is pairing up guy-girl. A few of the unlucky guys are stuck with each other. The girl that I wanted to be my partner is with someone else, but I'm glad to not be one of the unfortunate guy-guy pairings. Her friends giggle to themselves. Plotting and planning like a gaggle of high school hens. I'm too distracted with my own worries to care, to give it much thought.

She is a pretty woman. She is tall and statuesque, a Greek statue brought to life. She has brown hair cut at shoulder length. She has big doe eyes the color of the ocean after a storm. She is beautiful, but I don't care. I'm still thinking about the one I wanted to be my partner, the one who took cares to avoid being partnered with me. I know the woman standing in front of me. Her name is Helen. She is a fellow Portland hasher. She lives in the Hen House with Diva. I've been around her for a long time, but I've never really noticed her before.

The game is simple, erotic, and awkward. Each pair is given a banana and half a cantaloupe. Whip cream covers the banana and fills the cantaloupe. The man sits in a chair and holds the banana between his legs. The woman gets on her knees and removes the whip cream using only her mouth. They switch places. The cantaloupe goes between the woman's legs. The process is repeated with the roles switched. The first team to clean all the whip cream wins.

It's a fun game, an erotic game, but I don't really remember enjoying it. I'm not so dumb that I don't recognize the conniving of her friends. I'm distracted. Why is she doing this with me? Why isn't she doing this with Peyton? I know that Peyton is her boyfriend. I don't like Peyton. Peyton is a douche. He has a habit of talking to you, not with you. When he talks he only talks about the things he wants to talk about. They are not conversations, only lectures on the things that Peyton enjoys to do. You can try to change the subject, you can try to put in a word, but it is like trying to block a faucet with your hand.

It's hard to concentrate when your thoughts are on someone else, and when you can feel the eyes of jealousy boring into you from across the campfire. There are too many things to deal with. Too many loose strings. Why should I really care? There is something I want more. This is an unknown. This is something likely littered with trouble. Is Peyton her boyfriend or ex boyfriend? If he's an ex then it is recent. She rode up here with him, though granted, so did one of her friends. Who the hell would ride four hours with their recent ex? That's kind of fucked up. She seems awkward and she seems strange. This seems like a minefield best avoided. Never mind the fact that I've been fucking her cousin over the past few months.

The group goes for a run that afternoon. Up tree covered hills, down creek beds, along sandy beaches. We stop to rest in the grass next to a tall sea cliff, the water crashing on a beach far below. When we stop to rest, her friends work together again to make sure she's sitting next to me. They start conversations and try to suck us both into them, and then once words start moving back and forth, they disappear from the scene.

She seems fairly nice. I've never really talked with her before. She shows me how to make a blade of grass buzz by blowing across it. It's something I already know how to do, but I let her show me anyways. I make jokes to make her laugh. I like making people laugh. People like you when they laugh, they like you without really knowing you. She tries to flirt, but it is awkward. She is not very good at it. This is a fucking strange situation. I don't really know what to do, so I just go with the flow and ignore it at the same time.

Drinking. You can't have a hash camp out without drinking. From the very start of the morning it is socially acceptable to start drinking. You play games, take naps, go for runs, and steadily your amount of drunkenness increases. By the evening the world seems a more relaxed and easygoing place. It comes time for the ABC hash, the anything but clothes hash. Dress however you like or go naked. Just make sure nothing you wear could be considered clothes.

At the end many of us climb into the sauna, the stove is already piping hot. Naked bodies are shoved tightly together. I'm standing near the door. She comes in and stands next to me. She is naked, her nipples erect from the cold outside, the pasties that once made up her costume long gone. She still has the same shy and nervous look on her face she has had all day. She is obviously drunk, though I am drunk as well so it is not something I really notice. She stands looking at me and I catch my eyes running across the full length of her body before meeting hers.

"I'm naked."

Silence. It is a straightforward statement and completely true. It is an invitation, one that even somebody like me can recognize. I don't know what to say. What about Peyton? What about Melanie? What about the girl that only wants to be friends? So many strings in so many knots. My brain is slow and clumsy, overburdened by the beer that sloshes in my belly. I don't want to think right now. I don't want to bother. I don't want all these complications.

"Yes you are." I take a drink of my beer and look away. She looks at me a little longer, then walks back out into the night. I don't give it another thought. I raise my voice and make a joke, and ride the wave of dopamine from my fellow occupants' laughter. That was the right decision. It's better to avoid trouble whenever possible. That would have been nothing but trouble. But still, something, something about her.

Vanity

After her run, Devin stayed in the shower until the hot water ran out. She loved the warm embrace of the falling droplets, wrapping her in a world of relaxation and forgetfulness. Another place, before the slow collapse and then the sharp blast of cold forced her re-emergence into the authentic world. With hunched shoulders, she turned off the faucets and carefully acquired a towel, her movements quick and precise to displace as little of the shower curtain as possible in order to retain what whisps of the magic realm remained. The residue was patted away, not wiped, but patted, in order not to irritate her skin. The white terry cloth of the towel wrapped its way around her body, hugging the curves from the top of her breasts to the falling slope of mid-thigh. She admired her features in the still slightly steamy mirror. Her fingers found an eyebrow hair out of place, a little longer than its fellows. Pinched fingers removed the offender. A brush worked its way through her wet hair, undoing tangles and knots with sharp quick movements. Thus prepared, she emerged from the bathroom.

She could hear keys in the front door downstairs. The door coming open. Footsteps inside. The door closing. The sound of sniffed back snot. A grunt. A load falling from a shoulder to the floor with a heavy thud. Someone sitting down. A pair of cleats coming to rest. Sock covered feet making their way upwards, a beat as steady as that of her heart. Leo rose up the stairway. First his head, then his shoulders, and then all of him working its way into view. He looked tired. The salty residue of sweat clung to his brow. His baseball shirt and pants were both covered in dirt and grass stains. The Drunks, his rec league team name, was barely readable on the front. Devin flashed him a smile.

"Hi honey."

His eyes tracked across the dim light of the bedroom, fell on Devin for a moment, and then moved their way to the open bathroom door, steam still lurking around its upper edges.

"Any hot water left?"

"Sorry, I used it all. Should be more in about half an hour. Who won the game?"

Leo blinked, taking a moment to readjust his mind.

"We lost 4-5. I got tagged out sliding front ways into home."

Devin made sounds of interest to show that she was listening. Her back was already towards him, her front facing her dresser, her hands digging through to find something to wear. Leo stretched his arms behind his head and walked across the room. Devin made a selection of bra and panties, a cute matching set of lace, a selection that suggested that in her mind the house was not to be the final destination for the evening. She let the towel drop. Leo jerked open the curtains hiding the bedroom windows and pushed the windows open. They were big windows, nearly covering the one wall, facing out onto the street a story below. The light and sounds of the summer evening filled the bedroom. People talking. Passing cars. Squealing children. A cyclist moving by. Leo stood visible to the world and basked in its presence. Devin scrambled for her towel.

"What the fuck Leo?"

Leo turned, his face perplexed.

"What?"

"The curtains."

Leo turned his head to look at the offending hanging pieces of cloth. He turned back to Devin.

"What about them?"

Devin's face was cross, her eyebrows knitting harshly above her eyes.

"I'm naked."

"Yeah, so?"

"Maybe I don't want everybody to see me without my clothes on?"

"We're on the second floor. Who in the hell is going to see you?"

Devin gestured fiercely towards the house across the street.

"The neighbors."

Leo looked out the window and at the tan house with white trim across the way.

"Mr. Flanagan?"

"Yeah, for one."

"Mr. Flanagan is seventy years old. I'm pretty sure he's seen a naked woman before."

"He hasn't seen me naked."

Leo laughed. A sharp laugh that started high in the lungs and made a quick escape into the outside world. The laugh was accompanied by a shake of Leo's head. A shake that tried to whip off the clinging ridiculousness of the world. It was a harsh combination. A combination that made Devin want to slap Leo across his smirking face.

"Are you really that vain?"

Devin's eyebrows raised up a notch, registering her surprise.

"Vain?"

"Yeah, do you really think your such hot shit that some old man is sitting by his window all day, staring at our house, hoping to catch a glimpse of your hooters? There's a word for that, and that word is vanity."

Devin's eyes went wide and her mouth began to open, but Leo was too quick, guessing the direction she was taking, and taking advantage of her momentary shock.

"Now don't get me wrong. I find you very sexually attractive, but for you to try and tell me that everyone is just so desperate to see you naked that they're doing nothing but watching our house with fervent hope seems pretty damn ridiculous."

Devin was mad. Leo could tell that she was mad. Her forehead was crinkling, her head was jutting forward, and her hands were clenching and unclenching the way they always did when she got flustered.

"What if he just happens to be walking by his window Leo. What if someone just happens to be driving by?"

"I don't know. They probably say to themselves, hey look, a naked lady, and then keep right on driving. What do you think they're going to do? Stop their car? Get out a pair of binoculars?"

"Yeah, maybe."

"Fuck Devin. Nobody cares about your naked body. Everyone has the internet. I can pull my god damn phone out of my pocket and look up millions of naked ladies right now."

"Are you saying I'm not attractive?"

Leo rolled his eyes with exasperation.

"No, I'm not saying that. I'm just saying that you have to be pretty damn vain to think that you're so damn hot that some guy is going drive by in his car, see you naked, and suddenly be so overwhelmed that he has to pull over and start beating it right there. And I'll tell you what, if that ever happens, I'll go out and kick the guy's ass."

"What about Mr. Flanagan?"

"What about him?"

"What if he's jerking it?"

"Do you really think you got such great tits that a seventy year old man is going to suddenly lose control at the sight of them? Again, if he's doing it right in front of you, I'll go have words with him."

"What if he's behind his curtains?"

"What?"

"What if he's behind his curtains, jerking off?"

"Then who cares? You don't know he's doing it. Doesn't matter. None of your damn business. If that's all he's got, let him do it. Doesn't hurt you? Hell, if anything you ought to be flattered."

"Flattered? Really Leo? Fucking flattered? What if it was you?"

"Fuck Devin. I walk around naked with the windows open all the time. I obviously don't give a shit if someone sees my dick. You know why? Because I know it's just a dick. My dick's nothing special. It's no different than any other dick in the world. I mean shit, if someone wants to jerk off to my dick and I don't have to know about it, more power to them. None of my business."

Devin crossly roller her eyes.

"Oh, I'm sure the neighbors appreciate that."

"If it bothers them so much they can just close their curtains. It's just a dick."

"Maybe some of us want to keep our modesty."

Leo let loose with his laugh again. Devin's face turned bright red.

"Modesty. Are you seriously going to sit here and talk to me about your modesty? We were in Cancun last month with Katie and Kevin. You and Katie were butt ass naked on a beach full of strangers. For fuck sakes, the two of you were doing naked yoga. Don't give me this shit about your modesty."

"I'm not fucking vain. I just don't want everybody to see me naked."

"Jesus. Just the other day you were telling me about how men needed to quit sexualizing women's bodies, and now you're convinced that you're naked body is something super fucking special. Get your shit together."

Devin stiff marched forward and slapped Leo hard across the face. It felt good. She raised her hand again, but Leo grabbed her by the wrist. Her chest was heaving. Her heart was beating like mad. A palm shaped red mark was on his cheek. His left eyebrow twitched. They stood facing each other, staring eye to eye. Her whole body was quivering. Leo was smiling.

"Damn you're hot when you're angry."

Devin broke away and took a couple steps back towards the bed. She could see it in his eyes. The hunger.

"Oh no no no. You can just forget about that. There's no way you're touching this after all the shit you just said."

Leo shrugged.

"I'm a realist."

Leo took a step forward. Devin took another step back. There was a small sheen of sweat on her brow. The light breeze from the window felt good. Her eyes dropped to the growing bulge in his pants and then back up at his face.

"I'm not fucking vain."

The towel dropped to the ground. He was on her in an instant. Lips on her. Hands on her. They fell back entwined onto the bed, her anxious hands pulling at his clothing, helping him out of the confining layers. The world was dropping away in a rush, down into the depths of passion, but Leo broke away and raised his head above the surface.

"Hold on Devin. Let me close the damn window before we do this. I don't want the neighbors to hear us."

Evidence

Lisa sat bolt upright in bed. Paul lay on his side next to her, snoring softly. It had been a dream. Something about….no….it was gone. Lisa breathed in and let it out. Breathed in again, and let it out, unconsciously matching Paul's rhythm. What time was it? Her phone was on the floor next to the bed, plugged into the wall. It didn't really matter. It had just been a dream. Paul smacked his lips in his sleep and rolled onto his back. There was a faint trace of a smile on his lips. The spot under her right thigh was still damp. It had been a good night. She hadn't had a night like it in a long time. She hadn't known Paul could do things like that. He was in better shape now than she had remembered. Was she doing the right thing? Pressure in her bowels. She shouldn't have had the appetizer at dinner. There was always going to be trouble when she overstuffed herself. Perhaps it would fade. No. This was the real deal. Lisa pushed back the covers and swung her legs to the hardwood.

The house was pitch black. Lisa took baby steps, her hands out in front of her, hurrying as fast as she could. The pressure was growing. Bedroom doorway. Hallway. First door on the left. Bathroom. It was cold, but not uncomfortably so. Her hand fumbled for the light switch. Up the wall and back down. Once. Twice. The world painfully flashed into visibility. Sink. Bathtub. Tile floor. Lisa caught a brief glimpse of herself in the mirror. Bedraggled light brown hair. Mascara running. Hints of cellulite on her thighs. The toilet. The seat was down. Paul had never put the seat down when they were married. She had yelled and screamed, but he had never listened. A shift in her gut. No time to think about anything but the job at hand. Hike up her shirt. Paul's t-shirt, large on her frame, the Shamrock Run, last year. Panties down around her legs. A queen rests on her throne.

Lisa breathed a sigh of relief. Her eyes tracked across the tile of the floor and the beige paint of the walls. Waiting. Resting. What the hell was she doing? It all seemed so familiar. No, that wasn't fair. It felt different this time. The first time it had been like a fox run to ground after a long hunt. It had felt more like giving in. This time it felt nice, like getting home after a long vacation. Things were working out just fine. No problems. No issues. She could get up and go to bed, but it would mean being back in five minutes. She knew how these things worked. She wasn't a little girl anymore. The world was all out of surprises.

Lisa sat and waited. It didn't always happen, but it was best to be sure. She wished she had thought to bring her phone. She could play Candy Crush or maybe comb through Tinder. Was that wrong to do? To just look? There was something soothing about the judgement of the pictures. Swiping left and right. Ears too big. Too fat. Too skinny. Eyes too close together. You'd do in a pinch. Not in a hundred years. Possibilities. Thousands of possibilities. You never had to settle, but you never got to settle down. Life was short. There was more to it than short term thrills.

Lisa took a deep breath in and let it out. The bathroom stunk. She should really turn on the fan. No, it might wake Paul. She craned her head to look at the back of the toilet. No candles. No matches. That would be something she would have to rectify. Maybe a nice bath mat too. The one he had looked like an inheritance from the estate of a long dead relative, ratty and fraying at the edges. Boredom was setting in.

Lisa looked down in the garbage next to the toilet. Wads of Kleenex, strands of floss, and an empty box of store brand anti-diarrheal pills. At least it was something to read. Lisa reached down and picked up the box. Underneath was a razor, white with pink piping. It had a large round head. It was a woman's razor. Lori's razor. Lisa had never met the woman, only heard of her through mutual friends and Facebook posts, but there she was, sitting in the trash, winking with a knowing smile brought forth by the knowledge of their common bond. Gurgling in her stomach. Lisa put the empty pill box back in the garbage.

Things were on the move again. Lisa flexed her toes and stared down at the tile floor. Little white octagons speckled by lonely black ones near the walls. The grout was dirty. It needed a good scrub. A little elbow grease with a stiff brush. It sat by the bath mat, near the wall, a thin long black string. Lisa reached over and picked it up. She held it up to the light above to get a better look. It was black as night. A strand of Lori in her hand. Straight with a slight wave. Just like the smiling picture up at Tunnel Falls. She was being silly. It was just a hair, nothing more. Lisa slipped it between her legs so that it could be with the rest of the excrement. Nothing worth thinking about, soon to be flushed away.

There was another hair by the sink. Lisa reached over and put it in the toilet with its sibling. Another by the tub. One along the wall. Wait, another there as well. Lisa picked them up one by one, and dropped them all in the bowl to wait to be flushed away. Lisa wiped, it was time to go back to bed. No.

There were more. Three on the bathmat, tangled in with the fibers. Lisa picked them off, but found two more in the process. Lisa dropped down on her hands and knees, her panties still around her legs, her head down close to the tile. Hunting. Searching. Yes. There were more. A whole nest underneath the bath mat. A tangled tumbleweed amongst the dust bunnies behind the toilet. One stuck to the side of the sink pedestal. Jesus. How much hair could one woman lose? Was Lori bald?

They kept appearing, some in places Lisa swore she had already looked. They were breeding. Multiplying. All were added to the growing collection in the toilet. Lisa scoured every square inch of the bathroom. Top to bottom. Clean. Every surface had to be clean. She took a Kleenex and swept away the dust bunnies hiding near the walls, sweeping up more fine hairs in the process. One last hair. A light brown one. That one was okay. She let it retain its place on the bathroom floor. She looked down at the black rat's nest resting on top of the mass of wet toilet paper and Kleenex. Her finger pushed the flush handle. The water swirled and the mass was sucked down. Down into depths. Down to be forgotten.

What was she doing? Jesus. She was acting crazy. It was late. She needed to go to bed. Lisa pulled up her panties and looked at her profile in the mirror. She was getting older, but her tits still looked pretty good. Lisa washed her hands in the sink and rubbed some of the streaked mascara off her face. Maybe she'd repaint the bathroom. Seafoam. She'd always liked seafoam.

Lisa turned off the light and carefully felt her way back to the bedroom. Paul was snoring softly. She could just make out the darker patch in the blackness. Her hands came to rest on the edge of the bed. She laid down with her head on the pillow. She pulled up the sheet and blankets. Her fingers traced their way across the loose weave of one of the covers. Her eyes slowly shut. Her mind drifted. Her eyes snapped open. A hair. A hair between her fingers. Lisa moved slowly, not wanting to wake Paul. She reached down to her phone beside the bed. Her other hand brought the strand close to the floor. She hit the button, lighting the phone's screen. It was black. A black hair in the bed.

Bad Start

Leo had just gotten out of the shower when he heard the door slam downstairs. Devin was off to work. She had to get to work a half hour earlier than he did, which translated to a half hour earlier for everything in the morning. It was probably better that way, neither one of them were morning people. It helped keep the fights down, and lord knows they fought enough as it was. Leo toweled himself dry and used the back of his arm to wipe the steam off the bathroom mirror. His cheeks were a little stubbly, he might need to shave. They were always supposed to be clean shaven at work, but usually he could let it go a day or two between shavings and squeak by, at least most of the time. Sometimes if Don was in a bad mood he'd read Leo the riot act just so he'd feel like a big man, usually after a fight with his wife. Asshole. Fuck it, Leo would risk it today.

Devin started screaming outside. A loud cry of anguish that flipped on Leo's adrenaline switch. The towel around his waist dropped to the hallway floor. He rushed into the bedroom and pulled on his dirty shirt and pants from the night before. Down the stairs two at a time. In the living room the dog was up on the futon, darting from one side to the other in a panic. Leo didn't bother with shoes. He jerked open the door and rushed outside, careful to shut the door behind him to keep the dog inside.

It was a beautiful day. The sun was hanging cheerfully in a sky devoid of clouds. The air was comfortably warm. The rows of rented townhouses sat above the sidewalk on a short hill of grass. Parked cars lined the quiet street. Devin was wearing the green dress that showed off her figure. She sat in the gutter, clutching a mass to her chest, tears running down her cheeks tracing spider webs of mascara, head thrown towards the heavens, unleashing a torrent of horror and loss.

"Jimmy! God Jimmy no! My baby! My baby!"

Neighbors were peering out from behind their curtains. A car drove down the street, the driver slowing so he could rubber neck. Devin kept screaming. When Leo approached she held the lifeless form out to him, her arms shaking, snot hanging from her nose, her eyes taking nothing in, only spewing forth unbridled emotion.

"Look at him Leo! Look at him! I found him in the street! He's hurt! We have to help him! We have to help him Leo!"

There was nothing they could do. The big gray Maine coon was flat as a pancake and stiffened into a hairy board. Jimmy had probably been dead most of the night. Leo could still see the impression of the tire tracks across his back. Leo didn't know what to do, but he knew he had to say something.

"I'm sorry Dev, there's nothing we can do, I'm so sorry."

Devin collapsed into loud thick sobs, clutching the stiff dead cat, pressing her face into the coat matted with dirt and dried blood. Leo kneeled next to her, one hand on her shoulder, staring at the rows of townhouses. He caught the eye of one of their neighbors peering through their window. Leo shot the woman a dirty look. She broke eye contact and moved back out of sight.

"We have to get out of the street."

Devin didn't answer. She just kept crying, moistening the dried corpse with her tears. Leo helped Devin up and half dragged her to the grass where she collapsed again. He stood over her a moment, unsure what to do.

"I'll be right back. Okay?"

Devin nodded between fits and Leo went back into the house. The dog was worrying itself into a frenzy. It had already pulled the cover off the futon cushion, and was now jumping from futon to the floor, from the floor to the easy chair, and then back again. A never ending cycle of anxiety and growing destruction.

"Lay down."

Leo's voice was loud enough to echo off of the ceiling a bit. The dog collapsed mid-bound, falling to the floor where it curled into a tight ball and started whining. Leo went upstairs, reached for the towel on the floor, then thought better of it. It was his favorite towel. Leo lifted the towel and hung it back on the rack in the bathroom. He then got one of the old threadbare towels from the closet.

Back outside, Devin's cry of anguish had collapsed into a more sustainable blubbering, broken by the occasional squall. Leo's every move was slow and deliberate, a lone man near a dangerous beast. He gently took the dead cat from her arms, wrapped it in the towel, and took both it and Devin back into the house.

In the safety of the interior, Devin took back her baby in the towel and collapsed down on the futon. The dog got over and padded over, lying its black head on the cushion next to her. Devin pulled back the towel so the dog could see and sniff.

"Jimmy's dead Joey. Jimmy's dead."

Leo got Devin a couple tissues and a glass of water and sat down next to her. The tissues were quickly all used up, but did little to stop the flow. The glass of water was ignored, so Leo put it on the end table, safely away from the anxiety ridden dog. What the hell was he supposed to do now? Leo didn't have a lot of experience with this kind of thing. What do you do with a dead cat? Leo's first instinct was to just toss it in the dumpster, but he knew that was probably not going to be an acceptable idea. Were they going to have to go up to the woods or something? They'd have to get a shovel. Maybe he could borrow one. Leo was pretty sure Paul had a shovel.

"We have to take him to the vet."

Devin's words were pretty hard to understand. Leo had to have her repeat herself. They weren't much better the second time around, but Leo got the jist. The vet? What the hell was the vet going to do? The cat was dead. Even in her grief, Devin was a little psychic.

"Maybe the vet can help him."

Leo didn't bother to answer. There was a whole thing involved in answering that one which Leo had no desire to get into. It was pretty obvious that Devin wasn't all there right now. He'd have to be the responsible one. The vet probably wasn't a bad idea though. The vet was bound to be used to dealing with dead animals. Only problem was they had only been living in that part of town for the past three months. The old vet was clear across the city. That wouldn't work. He had to do something.

"Okay. I'm going to go finish getting dressed. You find the nearest vet on your phone."

That's the ticket. Get her doing something. Give her something to do. Leo went back upstairs, his head reeling, his body on automatic. Before he realized it, he was brushing his teeth in the bathroom. He hadn't planned on it. He just always brushed his teeth. He spit in the sink. The cat had always loved sitting in the sink. It would meow up at him until he either lifted it out or turned on the water for it. It had been part of the morning routine. Sometimes it would lick the faucet, which had always grossed Leo out. The cat had loved water. Often times it would jump in with Devin when she was showering. It had only done it once with Leo. The resulting reaction had guaranteed it would never happen again.

Leo put his shoes on in the bedroom. The comforter was covered in cat hair. Leo hated when the cat slept on the bed. The red lights of the alarm clock said 7:39. Shit. Work. Punch-in was at 8:00. Leo grabbed his phone off the dresser and pulled up the right contact. It rang five times before Don answered.

"Hello?"

"Don, it's Leo."

"What, you sick again or some bullshit?"

"No. I'm going to be a little late coming in today."

"What for?"

"My girlfriend's cat got run over last night."

"So what?"

"I have to take her to the vet?"

Silence on the other end. Leo chewed on the inside of his cheek.

"She's really upset."

Don coughed.

"Uh-huh. We're going to have to count it against your personal hours, plus you'll have to work late to catch-up."

"Whatever."

"See you when you get here."

The phone went dead. Dick. Leo went back downstairs. Devin was still on the couch crying, the dog licking the side of her leg where her dress had ridden up a bit. She looked like hell. Guessing that Devin probably hadn't looked up the nearest vet on her phone, Leo took care of it. The nearest vet was fifteen minutes away. At the very least it was in the opposite direction of the commuter traffic. Getting Devin into the car proved easier than he thought it would be. It was just a matter of gently pushing her in the right direction. He tried to take the towel from her, but she had a pretty firm death grip on it, so he wisely chose to let her be the sole bearer of that burden. They took his car. The smell of dead cat quickly filled the interior. Leo kept his mouth shut. He just rolled down the windows and kept driving. Devin mostly just cried quietly to herself. Occasionally Leo would rub her shoulder with his free hand, but he mostly had to use it for shifting. The car was a manual.

"I should have never let him outside."

Devin's words rattled hollowly through the cab. Leo kept his mouth shut and kept driving. It had been his suggestion that they start letting the cat out. The cat had always been more of an indoor cat, but from the moment they had moved into the townhouse, the cat had sat by the door and meowed late into the night. Nothing could get it to shut up. It had just meowed and meowed. It was a quiet neighborhood. The street wasn't that busy. There was plenty of grass in front and behind the rows of townhouses. It had seemed like it would be all right. Leo's entire was body was filled with tension, waiting for the other shoe to drop. It didn't. Devin started to cry again and Leo gave her shoulder another comforting squeeze.

The vet's office opened at 8:00. They got there at 8:14. The lobby was already half way filled with the usual assortment of sad looking cats and dogs, one guinea pig, and even a rabbit. Leo signed them in and led Devin to two chairs in a corner. They sat down. Leo put his arm around Devin. Her sobs were muffled, her face buried in the towel. Some people openly stared, even some of the other pets, but all looked quickly away when Leo glanced back at them. They sat that way for half an hour. People and pets would get called in, and then come back out and leave. New people and pets came in, providing new sets of eyes for another round of staring. Leo was relieved when the receptionist finally called Devin's name.

A tech led them back to the main examination room where a vet named Doctor Tibbetts shook their hands. The room smelled of shit and disinfectant. Somewhere in the bowels of the building a dog was barking. Everything about Tibbetts was average for a man in his late thirties. Average height, average going a little bit to fat, and average goatee. The vet took the towel from Devin, carefully placed it on the examination table, and unwrapped its contents. He was silent as he looked over the flattened cat in the medical grade lighting.

"Hmmmm. Yes, he is most certainly dead."

Devin choked back another sob. Leo didn't like the vet's tone. It was so matter of fact that it almost sounded like parody. The vet continued on, oblivious to Devin's reactions.

"I'm so sorry for your loss."

Leo didn't think the vet sounded all that sorry, but god only knows how many times the man had to say it in a day.

"We'll cremate the body. Will you be wanting to keep the ashes?"

Devin nodded her head.

"The cost will be forty to eighty dollars."

Leo couldn't help himself. He had to ask.

"What's the difference between forty and eighty?"

The vet didn't bat an eye.

"For eighty we'll cremate your pet separate. For forty we put it in with all the other animals that died today and then give you an equivalent amount of ash."

Son of a bitch. Devin started crying again, big heavy sobs, choking the words between the intakes.

"Keep him separate. Keep my baby separate."

The vet nodded. Leo wanted to punch him in the teeth, but restrained himself. It sure as hell wouldn't help anything right now. Devin was standing over the body. Her hand stroking the soiled gray fur.

"Can I have a moment to say goodbye."

The vet nodded.

"Of course."

The vet and Leo stepped out into the hallway. The tech led a dog and worried looking man past them into another examination room. Devin came out after a few minutes. Her eyes were bloodshot and filled with tears, but she wasn't sobbing anymore. The vet led them back to the front desk.

"You can pick up the remains any time tomorrow during business hours. If you don't claim the ashes in thirty-six hours we'll dispose of them. Sorry again for your loss."

The vet disappeared back into the bowels of the clinic. The too chipper receptionist ran Devin's credit card. As they were leaving the tech caught them at the door.

"Didn't want you to forget your towel."

Devin took the threadbare towel and held it tightly the whole way home.

"I shouldn't have let him go outside."

Leo took a breath in and let it out.

"He wanted to go outside. He was happier going outside."

"I know. I just miss him so much already."

"He was one hell of a cat."

Leo didn't mean it. He had never been much of a pet person, but it seemed like the right thing to say.

"I've read before that you can get the ashes made into a diamond, or that you can get them mixed with ink for a tattoo. I think I'll do that. Then I'll always have him with me."

Leo nodded, but didn't say anything. They sounded like stupid ideas to him. Jesus, it was just a cat. Saying so wouldn't help any though. It would make things worse. She was pretty emotional at the moment, it would take a bit for her to get her head back on straight. Either way, it would probably be better than having to stare at a cat urn on a shelf.

The moment they walked through the door of the townhouse, Devin began gathering up all of the cat stuff. Feeding dishes, scratching post, laser pointer, feather on a string, cat house, everything. She even swept up as much of the cat hair as she could, of which there was no shortage. All of it was packed out and thrown into the dumpster. Leo thought about saying something, but kept his mouth shut. The look of stubborn determination on Devin's face was frightening. Instead, he dutifully helped her carry everything out, though when she wasn't looking, he slipped a jingle ball into his pocket. She'd probably want it later. He'd give it to her when she started to regret throwing everything out. She had loved that cat. She'd probably want something to remember it by.

Once everything was in the dumpster, Devin collapsed down onto the futon. The dog jumped up next to her and put its head in her lap. Leo had long since given up trying to keep the animals off the furniture. It was 10:35. Leo needed to get to work.

"You going to be okay?"

"Yeah, I think so."

"Okay. I'm going to head to work."

"I'm probably going to skip work today."

"Okay. Let me know if you need anything."

Leo went upstairs and changed into his work clothes. By the time he came back down Devin was rolling a joint. Leo didn't say anything about it. It was another one of her needs he just didn't understand, like letting the animals up on the furniture, or treating them like children.

"I'll see you this evening."

"Okay."

Devin lit the joint as Leo closed the front door behind him. Leo wished she would at least smoke outside. He hated it when she stunk up the townhouse. It didn't matter right now though. It wasn't a good time for that battle. Let her get high in peace. Leo got into his car and cranked up the motor. He pulled out into the street and headed for work. She had been high the night before too, when she drove home after hanging out all evening with Katie. She was always out getting high with Katie. Leo had been watching television when he heard her drive up. He had heard the car parking, a thump, and then she had walked in about a minute later, giggling and still floating through the air. Leo shook his head. That was one he planned on taking to the grave. His father hadn't raised an idiot.

Respite

A few simple thoughts, a daydream, a mind set free to wander where it will. The mind wanders into areas where I do not want it to go. I try to stop it, to call it back and force it into safer places, but the mind rebels. The mind wants to venture forth into the dangerous world, to abandon the walls that make it safe. I try to pull it back harder, to focus on other things. I try to make it avoid the thoughts and memories that fill me with pain. The harder I fight the harder my mind fights back. I try to think of anything else. I think of topics from work, memories of my childhood, books I've read, memorized lists, anything but her. I have lost control of my mind, I am not its master, it has become mine.

I lay awake in my bed, tired, but sleep won't come. Something is going to happen, every instinct in my body is screaming for me to be ready for the coming danger. Adrenaline courses through my veins. Every beat of my heart echoes in my ears, the chugging of my internal engine. All of my muscles are tense, flexed as hard as they can flex, trying to make my prone body look bigger than it is. Something is out there, something that can hurt me, I have to be ready. I lay on my back, yet I can still run my hand underneath me. My muscles pull my spine into a curve. Only my ass and my shoulders touch the mattress. The muscles in my back ache, the strain is too much for them.

I shake, a tiny imperceptible vibration. It is like a constant electrical shock coursing through my body. Every cell is vibrating and I'm powerless to control them. I hold my hand in front of my face. I can see it shaking. I can see the tension. The potential energy of my body has reached the point where it can no longer be completely contained. I have to be ready, have to watch out, something is going to happen. I can feel my toes and fingers curling involuntarily. There is a need, my body has a need, to jump up and run around the house like a madman. Our bodies are not designed to contain such energy, it must be released. I have to be prepared. I have to be ready.

My mind is in a panic, it can see no danger, see no trouble. My body is setting off every alarm bell, calling everyone to battle stations. My mind is desperately trying to catch up. Searching. Searching. What the hell is the problem? Why do I feel like I'm about to explode? What is going on? What is happening to me? None of it makes sense. I have to do something. My mind desperately tries to figure out what that something is. Fight or flight, the most basic commands of the brain. My body is telling me to fight or flee, but my mind can't figure out what I'm supposed to fight or flee from.

Panic. None of it makes sense. Nothing makes sense. I desperately try to divert my mind to other thoughts. To force my body to relax, but I'm powerless. I'm confused. I'm scared. I feel like I must be insane. The potential energy in my body continues to build. The slight vibrations get stronger. The vibrations turn into shakes. I can feel my entire body trembling on the bed. There is nothing I can do. I have no control over myself. I can feel the layers of my sanity begin to peel back. I can feel the barriers that I have built to protect the world within which I live collapse before the onslaught of my own subconscious. I'm insane. I must be insane. My eyes fill with tears of frustration and fear. I just want it to end. I'd do anything to make it end. Please god make it end. Why? Why? Why?

Silence. I lay in a bed much too big for me, the blankets stretch out as far as the eye can see in all directions. I wear an old pair of pajamas made of flannel, made by my mother. She made them on the sewing machine that sat in her room. My mother used to always make things when I was a child. The pajamas were hand me downs, worn first by my older brother. When he outgrew them they got passed down to me. When I outgrow them they will be passed down to my little brother.

I feel tiny in the bed, an insignificant dot. So tiny and insignificant that no trouble can be bothered to haunt me. I lay relaxed and safe, my body warm and encased in my little cocoon of cotton and wool. My head lays on a cool pillow. A soft breeze from the window ruffles my hair. A small white blankie is clutched in my tiny arm. I lay half asleep without a single trouble on my soul. I lay relaxed and calm. There are no fears and no doubts.

My back begins to ache, right between my shoulders. I can feel my shoulder blades begin to be drawn closer together. The bed shrinks around me, or is it me growing? Monsters begin to climb from the depths from which I had banished them. Dark monsters with no shapes or substance. Worries, fears, doubts. I feel them all begin to flood back in. I can feel the paradise around me begin to slip away. I can feel my body begin to tense again as it prepares to fight the escaping monsters. The feelings of safety, relaxation, and calm flee before the coming onslaught. They are but memories, the moment but a dream.

*   *   *

The alarm begins to blare, throwing me from my sleep. I awaken, sweating in my bed. My toes are curled slightly and I have to make a conscious effort to uncurl them. My back is sore and tight, especially my right shoulder. As I blink my eyes the last visages of my paradise slip away and are gone. I get out of my bed and climb into the shower. The hot water pounds on my back, but does little to loosen the tightness. I eat breakfast and take an over the counter pain killer with my usual series of vitamins and allergy pills. I get dressed and I drive to work.

I concentrate on what I need to get done today. I turn on the radio to provide further distraction, careful to avoid radio stations that might play songs that remind me of the ghosts of the past. I feel drained, exhausted. The walls were breached, but by some miracle I have survived the night. It's only a matter of time. But it's only a matter of time before the distractions are all finished. Work will get done, social events will come to an end. It's only a matter of time before I'm alone again with the beasts that inhabit my mind. The day goes as expected.

I wake up in the morning with a hangover. I've been running a lot, hashing as many times a week as I can. It's an escape, an escape from my reality. For just a brief amount of time I can be around people without troubles or problems. For a short amount of time I can forget all of the pain, all of the confusion, all of the regret. For just a short amount of time I can get drunk and pretend I am still the man I once was. I'm numb inside, I don't feel anything. My body goes through its morning routine on automatic. Get up, shower, eat breakfast, get dressed, drive to work. My body is moving without a driver. My mind has retreated into the nether regions of my consciousness. Retreated to a place where it hopes to be safe.

From the very first moment that I awaken my mind begins to play through the troubles and the grief. The first thing I see in my head as my mind slowly comes back awake is her. The confusion washes over me in a wave of questions. What happened? Why did she act the way she did? Was it something I did? Was it something wrong with me? What is she afraid of? Anxiety. The only reason I could ever get out of her ebbs and flows upon the current. A single word meant to explain a complex troubled psyche. A single word that has left me only with more questions. Questions that will never be answered. Anxiety. What did she mean by anxiety?

My brain shifts and tries to make sense of things that it does not, and cannot understand. Anxiety. What was going on? Perhaps it was just an excuse, a cowards way of avoiding true answers. Did it have to do with Peyton? Was she still in love with Peyton? When I looked into her eyes did she still think about him? When I held her in my arms did she wish it was him instead of me? Did it have to do with Melanie? Did it have to do with Melanie and the looks she'd give me? The looks that I told myself over and over again were just looks? The looks that I knew and recognized? The looks that I told myself to ignore? Was her relationship with Melanie being destroyed by her relationship with me?

I try to distract myself by thinking of anything else, anything at all. In my head I count and go through lists memorized long ago. I cannot escape it though. I cannot escape all of the painful loose ends. All of the unanswered questions. Does she care about me? Did she ever care about me? Why does she pretend that it was all nothing? Why does she treat me as though I am nobody? What happened? Anxiety. Anxiety. Anxiety. I don't understand.

On my car ride to work I turn on the radio and turn it up until it drowns out the thoughts in my head. Music, music will soothe the restless soul. I never realized before how many songs involve falling in love or losing love. It seems like all of them are somehow based upon this theme. I quickly turn the radio over to a news station. I listen to an editorial on the current financial budget crisis of the federal government. I conjure up arguments both pro and con to the outlined debate. Anything to distract myself. Anything to try and forget.

The rain begins to fall in a random drip drip upon my windshield. The sky is gray and bleak, overcast by clouds that give the promise of darkness and dreariness. I turn on my windshield wipers and watch raindrops smear across the glass. I feel nothing. I have to feel nothing. If I let myself feel anything I just feel despair. Sometimes I feel bouts of happiness, sometimes I can throw myself so into something that I forget. Sometimes I feel bouts of anger. I throw myself into a rage. That bitch, that bitch had no right to do this to me. She had no right to treat me the way she treated me. She had no right to do the things she did. What wasn't she telling me? But the anger always subsides. It always bubbles forth in a great explosion, leaving a gaping hole that is quickly filled by the despair. I feel sad for myself. I feel sad for her. I feel trapped and alone. Anxiety. What was she trying to tell me?

My car climbs the steepening road to pass over the hills into downtown to reach my work. I stop at a light and see a young couple holding each other at the bus stop. They are gazing at one another and laughing. They see only each other. I hate them. I deplore them. I curse them for their happiness and ability to be carefree. I hate myself for hating them. There is no one I can curse, there is no one I can hate. I cannot hate myself. How can you hate someone who broke under such pressure? I cannot hate her. How can you hate someone who is trapped and scared, a prisoner of their own mind? I try again to believe that everything she told me was complete bullshit. I try to hate her for fucking with me. I try and I fail. I try to hate those around her. I try to hate the whole world, but I cannot. I cannot hold onto it long enough. Sadness and despair flow back into the emptiness.

I do not want to think about it, but my mind is no longer under my direct control. If I'm doing something I am fine. If I can concentrate on a task I can function like a normal happy person, but it's the times that I am alone, the times that I have my thoughts to myself. These are the times that I cannot escape. These are the times that the thoughts come flooding back in. Anxiety. A single word that held all the answers. A single word I cannot understand.

The car moves along the road. On my left is hillside, on my right a drop to the creek below. I look at the drop. If I turned the wheel slightly the car would change the direction of its forward velocity. If I turned the wheel slightly things would be very different. I banish the thought. Banish it to the dark depths and recesses of my mind where I hide the most obvious signs of madness. I know that I don't want to die. I want to live. I want to see tomorrow. I don't want to hurt myself. I don't want to punish myself for past misdeeds. I just want a distraction. I just want something to happen. Something that will break the terrible never ending cycle that I have found myself caught in. Anxiety. What is the meaning of the word? Was I wrong with everything I felt? It didn't seem like it at the time. Maybe it was. Maybe I was insane. Maybe I'm going insane. Maybe I am insane.

The car drive ends without incident. The thought is banished. I arrive safe and sound. A quick walk through the rain to the door. Inside and up the elevator. First one to arrive in the office. Boot up my computer and begin opening programs. The morning routine, safe, familiar. The morning routine, automatic, no distractions. There is nothing very close to pending today. There is nothing that has to get done right at this moment. The just sitting around is killing me. I open up Facebook and look at her page. I will probably do it several more times throughout the day. I know I shouldn't, but I can't help it. I need to feel busy. I need to feel like I'm doing something to solve the problem. My mind won't let me just sit and do nothing. Obsession. She used the word once. It had hurt. Of course I'm obsessed. I had everything I ever wanted violently jerked away from me by a single word. Anxiety.

This is pointless. This is worthless. This does nothing to help. My eyes cloud with uncried tears and I quickly close the internet browser, angry at my foolishness, angry at my weakness, angry at my inability to do anything about my problem. I am afraid. I am a coward. I cannot express myself. I cannot do anything. It's all too much. My coworkers begin to arrive. I throw myself into my work. My job requires me to think. My job requires my mind to be focused. I spend the morning distracted. My productivity is at an all time high.

The thoughts return as I walk to lunch. I cannot escape them. I can't get away. I eat lunch and read a comedy website. I read and laugh. I can't let my mind wander. I can't let it roam free. It always returns to the place where I do not want it to go. Anxiety. *Five Myths About The Dark Ages.* Anxiety. *Man In Louisiana Kills Gator With Bare Hands.* Anxiety. *Top Ten Ways To Fix The Economy.* Anxiety. I check Facebook, relishing in the artificial feeling of connection. Trying to understand what happened. Why? Why? Why? Why?

I don't have any work to complete in the afternoon. I have been too productive in the morning. Everything that I can get done is already done. The internet holds no distractions for me. Billions and trillions of points of information and I can find nothing to hold my interest. Nothing to keep me distracted. I have always been sluggish in the afternoon. I was not born to get done with lunch and just sit at a desk. I was born to work, physical exertion, the feeling of euphoria to see a job done. I sit in my chair and only think of depression. I sit in my chair and only think of the horrible things that I saw, and the horrible things that I did. Anxiety. Guilt, anger, sadness. I have been cast off and abandoned.

Dark clouds pour over the hills and into the downtown of the city. The sprinkle of rain increases into buckets. Great sheets of water fall from the sky and drench all that they touch. The river churns beneath the onslaught. Blowing winds throw the precipitation so thickly against my window that my view is obscured. I stop all that I am doing and stare at the world outside my office. The walls and window hold the storm at bay, they make me no longer part of the world with all its storms and deluges. Anxiety. Anxiety. Anxiety. I do not understand.

My exhausted mind goes blank, the synapses quit firing. It feels like I stare out the window for only five minutes or so, drinking in the onslaught, feeling the storm of my mind collapsing into silence before the power of the world around me. Blankness. Emptiness. Nothingness. When I look back up the storm has gone, the clouds have broken, and blue sky peaks through the gray gloom. The work day is over. I do not remember the hours that have passed by. I gather my stuff and leave. My body moves on automatic, no thoughts run through my head. I get in my car and drive home. I change into my running clothes and drive out to the hash. I socialize, I run, I drink more than I should. I drive myself home. I lay down in my bed and wait for sleep to take me.

I am not alive. I am not dead. I am just here. I feel like I am not here. I feel like I am a long ways away from the world around me. There are walls and a window I cannot see. It is soothing. It is soothing to feel nothing. To feel like you are not part of the world. I cannot live my life this way. I cannot let myself become a prisoner within myself, but for now I let the peacefulness wash over me. For now I take the respite from my pain, and escape.

I lay in bed as the first rays of morning light stretch through the window. I am in that point between being asleep and being awake. My brain moves independently, out of my control. It wanders and creates things out of nothing. It is free to roam and I can only lay and watch it. I am not awake enough to force my mind to move in the direction that I wish it to.

I can see her in my mind. Tall, lithe, and beautiful. I can see over time the anger and hurt subsiding. I can see her slowly start to understand the things I tried to say. Understand the reason behind all the things I tried to do. I can see her standing up and facing down her problems. She moves out of the Hen House, she gets away from those people who offer a comfort that only holds her back. I can see her going to a therapist and fighting the battles that need to be fought.

One day I run into her, both of us walking down the street. I don't look away. I don't hide as I know I probably would in reality. I say hello and she says hello back. It's awkward. We make stilted small talk for just a minute or two, both of us are uncomfortable, and then we separate and move apart again. I can feel my anxiety rising and I can imagine hers doing the same as well, but I notice that there has been a change. I see the change in her. She is no longer shaking. The anxiety is there, but it no longer controls her. She is no longer running away from it. She is meeting it head on. It has been reduced from a crisis to just another emotion.

I feel a sense of elation. Accomplishment. A feeling that it has all been worth it. The sadness of the loss is still there, but at least I know it wasn't for nothing. As we walk away from each other she turns and says my name. I turn back.

"I'm sorry," she says, "I'm sorry for how I treated you."

I give a plaintive smile. "It's all right."

"You tried when nobody else would. You tried even when you knew it would cost you everything. Thank you."

My smile, somewhat forced, becomes entirely real. I feel so many words try to get out at once. So many emotions come bubbling to the surface. It is overwhelming. I feel myself begin to cry, in both the fantasy and in reality. They are the tears of someone who has fought a long battle. They are the tears of someone who has long ago given up hope, but still secretly holds a small piece of it deep inside themselves. They are the tears of someone who never believed they would be in this place. The feeling is contentment.

I jerk myself out of the dream. I force myself out before the people in my imagination fulfill all of my secret desires. It's just a fantasy world. It's not real. I have to live in the real world. I know what will happen next. I do not want to see that look in her eyes that I once remembered. I do not want to hold her in my arms and feel her hold me back. I do not want to go farther down this road.

The rational part of my brain knows that the farther I travel, the farther it gets from the possibility of reality. I throw my own hopes and desires away. Just knowing that her life is better. Just knowing that the monster no longer controls what she thinks or what she does. That is enough. That is enough to hope for. The rest. The rest is just fantasy. I lay in bed a few minutes more, and let the thoughts I do not let myself think trickle like sand through my fingers. For just a moment I let myself hold onto the feelings of bliss and contentment. Then I let them fall. I get up. I start my day.

I wake up in my bed alone, my stomach growls with indigestion. It's still dark outside, I don't need to wake up for another 3 to 4 hours. My apartment is quiet around me, the world holds still, waiting for the breaking of the dawn. I roll over and try to sleep. Familiar thoughts begin to snake through my brain. These thoughts come often, they fill my mind, they have become the core of my being. When my brain is focused, I can direct my thoughts like a torrent from a firehouse, but when I let my thoughts settle, my mind wanders on its own, to the subject that inevitably bubbles to the top.

Sometimes the thoughts are anger, railing against the world that I have found myself in. Anger against her, what she did to me, her foolishness, her mistakes, how she is hurting herself. Anger against her friends, their selfishness, their cowardice, their inability to help her, their unwillingness to help me. I imagine myself yelling at her. Yelling at them. Breaking through the walls they've built by sheer force and volume. Anger against the world in general, the selfish uncaring world that would let such a person have such things happen to her. Sometimes it is anger against myself. Anger at my mistakes. Anger at my own failings. Anger for letting myself fall as far as I have. The anger is hot and burns out quickly. A sudden explosive burst that collapses back downward into a general feeling of sadness. The anger is a gorilla rattling against its cage, attacking the bars and pounding its chest, but then falling to the ground tired and exhausted, its energy used up, still stuck.

Sometimes the thoughts are hopeful. Sometimes I lay there awake and put all that I have learned together. I put together solutions and start thinking diplomatically. I begin looking for ways to explain all that I have learned, to express the hope I have found in the knowledge for better days ahead. Within my head my words are like honey and wine. They are logical, they are persistent, they are convincing. I have no need to batter down the door, for they open it and come out to me. A thousand speeches never said out loud. A thousand arguments never entered into the debate. Logic is pointless in such instances. Logic has no place in a problem that is illogical. Sometimes the hopeful thoughts center on the repair of my own self-doubts. You're doing the right thing. Everything is going to be all right. You're going to be all right. Hope lasts longer than anger, but in the end it sinks into the same pit of despair.

Sadness and despondency, these are the foundations of all other thoughts of her. Sadness and despondency are the bedrock upon which my psyche now sits. In the end, when the hope has been lost and the anger subsides, I always return to sadness. A feeling of great loss, memories of what I had and what is no longer here. A feeling of helplessness. You cannot control the world around you, and you most certainly can't control others. All the anger, all the planning, all the hope, all pointless because she has given up the fight long ago. It's strange to sit covered by a blanket of malaise. To know that there is nothing you can do. To feel all of the fight seep out of you because it is a fight you cannot win. Your mind sits in the past and remembers. Old wounds and half healed scars are ripped open. Memories of the loss, avoided for so long. Memories of the mistakes, how things could have been different if you had just known more at the time.

Tears roll down your cheeks. Time, sacrifice, love. A piece of you is gone and you do not know how to get it back. You are not the man you once were. You have fought, you have been beaten, and you have paid a terrible price. You can never go back to who you once were. You can never be anyone but who you are now. You are the prizefighter, your brain pummeled until it is slow and jerky. Remembering all that you have accomplished and feeling a great sense of pride, but seeing how you are now and wondering if it was worth it.

You are alone. You have long ago given up trying to tell people about what happened. You couldn't make them understand. You couldn't get them to see why you did the things you did. Why you just couldn't walk away. You are alone in this. You have no one to talk to. No one to reassure you. There is one thought that is worse than all the others. One thought that is the most frightening. One thought that causes the most anxiety. Even as you fight to break through, cracks of self-doubt begin to bring down the walls of your own reality. You cannot examine the brickwork of another's defenses without seeing the weaknesses in your own. We all have an inner self, a hidden part of us that we hide from those around us. We all have an inner self, an even more hidden part of us that we hide from ourselves.

What if I am the one who is crazy? A friend once described for me what it meant to be around someone who is crazy. You're riding in a car with them and you get to a green light. It's obvious that it's a green light, everyone knows that it's a green light. Yet your friend stops, to them it's a red light. You try to tell them to go, but they won't. No matter how you try to debate and argue they do not see what is obvious to everyone else. They see a red light. It seems so simple, so cut and dried, but it's not.

What if you have never talked with anyone about green lights? What if in your entire life you have avoided the subject of green lights whenever it has come up? What if the entire subject of what color the light is makes you and everybody around you uncomfortable, so nobody ever talks about it? You pull up to the green light, your friend says that it's red. How can you prove that they are wrong? How can you prove that your perceptions are not the ones that have been skewed?

Even if you talk to friends about what color the lights are, you never say everything that is on your mind. What if the parts you hold back are the parts that show you are wrong? What if the only reason they agree with you is because you did not tell them the entire story? What if in all the times you discussed stoplights you never once mentioned the colors? What if your friends don't really agree with you but are being nice because they care about you? They don't want to hurt you. What if they perceive that being your friend and letting you see the light as red is better than possibly losing your friendship and forcing you to go through severe psychological trauma as the delusion is pulled asunder?

Imagine yourself as this person. How would you react when one person stands up and tries to tell you the light is green? One person who doesn't want to see you get hurt in an accident caused by constantly stopping at intersections you don't need to stop at. Imagine. Who would you listen to? All your life you have seen the light is red, and no one has ever told you anything different, then one lone crazy person pops up and says that you are wrong. You may have your own doubts. You may notice that you are the only car that is stopping at the intersection. You may watch all the other cars drive through without stopping and wish you could just blow right through too, but the light is red to you, it has always been red to you. Which is easier, to rethink how you perceive reality and examine the cracks in your psyche, or to see the one person who is willing to speak up as a lunatic?

What if I am the crazy one? I'm self aware enough to know that I am not infallible. I can think back to many points in my life where my brain has managed to trick itself, managed to distort the world around me to match its perception of reality. What if I'm the crazy one? What if all I perceive is distorted by a sick brain desperate to hide the truth from itself? What about my memories? What of all the things I remember seeing, all the things I remember her, and others, saying? Don't they prove that I am sane? The brain is a powerful instrument. It will do anything to protect itself. What if the way I remember things are not the way they were at all? I am alone. She will not talk about these things. Her friends only give hints and riddles. My friends call her crazy, but they only know her through what I've told them. What if I am the one who is crazy?

It is a horrifying thought, a terrible thought to have in a fit of insomnia at three in the morning. You have no one to hold you, no one to comfort you, no one to tell you it's going to be okay. Even if I did, I don't know if I'd necessarily want them to. Not if it was only to rebuild the wall of my own delusions and fantasy. In some ways it is a comforting thought. It's a comforting thought to be the crazy one, not her. Months of worrying about her and her problem could vanish without a trace. The problem would be mine, not hers. Nothing would be wrong with her. Nothing would be in the way of her being happy. The battles would be mine, she would not have to face them. It's a comforting thought to think I'm crazy, to take all the problems onto myself, both hers and my own.

I'm not crazy. I have problems, and I have things that I need to work on. I have made mistakes and miscalculations. I have let my mind go into the realms of unreality at times, but I am capable of finding my way back. Brick by brick I rebuild. I'm not the crazy one. I'm doing the right thing. My memories are not false, they are not imagined. I'm not crazy. The things I saw and heard were real, but maybe I am crazy in the way I'm dealing with it. Maybe I am crazy. Where am I crazy and where am I not? A frightening set of thoughts.

My alarm clock begins its incessant buzzing. I get up, get dressed, shower, shave, and brush my teeth. I head out the door to work. In the car I turn on the radio to drown out the thoughts within my head. Soon I'll be at work, soon I'll have distractions. Brick by brick, the wall guarding my reality is rebuilt. Slowly but surely the self-doubts are pushed back into the wilderness from whence they came, but it's impossible to banish all of them. Not all can be hidden back away. They remain in the back of my mind, a nagging feeling that perhaps the walls have been built too high. That perhaps on certain fronts they need to come down. My car travels up the same familiar roads, and I sit and wish for the silence of sleep.

A Good Old Fashioned Ash Whooping

It all started when the tree hit me. One moment I'm floating on a nice buzz, next thing you know, bam, down on my hands and knees. It was a beautiful day, so when I got home from work I decided to go out for a run. By beautiful, I mean just perfect. Bright sunshine. A little cool breeze. Just the thing to put a little verve in your motor. I don't know, lately I've just been spending my evenings watching old episodes of *Seinfeld* on Hulu, but something about that day just lit a spark under my ass. Before I even got home the whole idea formed in my head. Get home, change, run down to Gigantic, have a beer, run back. A nice three mile run all together.

Usually I run alone, but something in me just itched to reach out to see if anybody else wanted to go. Like I said, there was just something in the air. I felt like an old cow that had been locked in the barn all winter, suddenly turned into a frolicking calf when the barn doors are opened in the spring. Anyways, I sent a text to Nick to see if he'd like to come. Good guy Nick. Always up for a run or a beer, or the two combined if needed.

Bastard probably runs everyday. It only took six minutes or so to get ready. Shoes, shorts, and my favorite tech shirt. The one with the hole in it. It's damn hard to find a running shirt with a good fit. My shoes were going a little smooth, but I hadn't had time to get new ones. If I ran too long in them they'd make my knee hurt, but I wasn't going that far. I didn't hear a damn thing back from Nick, though to be fair, I didn't give him all that much time. Whatever, I didn't feel like waiting. I had that much need to just get up and go.

Keys and a ten dollar bill in my pocket and I was out the door. No phone. I've been trying to carry my phone around less. I don't like how I'm always checking it all the time. The run down was nice, probably because it was almost entirely downhill. Every step felt like I was flying. Every step felt like it was launching me ten feet up into the air, up and over the roofs of all the houses. On my way down I swerved a bit off course just to run by Nick and Phoebe's house. Didn't see anybody. I thought about going up to the door and knocking, but I didn't. I don't know, it probably shouldn't have felt weird, but for some reason it did.

Anyways, after having to convince myself that I hadn't gotten lost, I got down to Gigantic, and you know who was there? That's right. Nick and Phoebe sitting on that old couch in the corner. They raised their beers and I waved and then gestured that I was going to get in line and grab a beer before sitting down. It turned out that Nick and Phoebe were already down there when they got my text, but I had left before they had responded. However, I didn't know that until I sat down. First I had to go through the beer line, which was slow as shit thanks to some woman ahead of me needing to try every beer they had on tap. A situation that wasn't helped any by the fact that the bartender, an aging punk fan with an infectious laugh, was more than happy to recite a full volume of information for every small glass she served. This left me with an uncomfortable amount of time to stare at my surroundings, which wasn't much given that Gigantic is pretty much just a big shed with a garage door. I mostly looked at the art hanging by fishing line from the ceiling, mostly zeppelins made out of beaten copper, and avoided looking over at Nick and Phoebe. Nick caught me looking over once, so I pretended to look at an imaginary watch and mimed an exasperated sigh.

Once I finally got my beer I made my way over and sat down in a chair next to them. We of course had the usual pleasantries, the asking what beer each of us had gotten, and the offering of sips from each other's glasses. You know, the Portland version of a hello kiss on the cheek. There were of course the usual "how are you doings" with the of course required "fines", though of course I really wasn't fine, but it really wasn't anything I wanted to get into. Things got a little awkward when Phoebe asked how Devin was doing. It was nothing malicious, just a force of habit. Luckily, Nick maneuvered us nicely out of it by mentioning that he and Phoebe were going to DC the next week.

This set the discussion onto a whole new tangent. Phoebe had never been to DC before, and she was pretty damn excited to be going. Nick hadn't been since he was in high school. They wanted my opinion on where to go so I of course suggested the Holocaust Museum and the Postal Museum. Whenever anyone says they're going to DC I always suggest those two. The Holocaust Museum is really well put together, though you'll probably cry for about an hour after getting out, and well, the Postal Museum is much cooler than you think it would be.

Anyways, after finishing our beers Nick and Phoebe excused themselves so they could go get some dinner, Phoebe is not the kind of person you want to be around when she's hungry, and I started jogging back up to my house. I was maybe half a mile in when a kick ass looking metallic orange El Camino drove by, drawing my eye, and it was right when I looked back in front of me that the hard gnarly claw of that fucking ash tree reached out and smacked the top of my head.

Dazed is probably the right word for how I felt, though my head hurt pretty bad too. I never blacked out or anything. I mostly remember running and then just being on my hands and knees, blood dripping on the ground. I raised my hand to check my head and it came back slathered with blood. The flow went from a couple drips to a pretty impressive flow fairly quickly. Not knowing what to do, but recognizing I had to do something, I stood up and reached up again to check how big of a hole I had in my noggin. It wasn't really a pleasant feeling. I could tell there was a pretty good gash in my head, but I couldn't really tell how big. It was all pretty slick up there, never mind the blood rapidly covering my face and clothes. This wasn't something I was going to be able to handle on my own, especially given that I was still a mile from home.

Not really having many other options, I decided the best idea would be to start knocking on doors and asking for help. I didn't really know how this was going to go given that I looked like I was straight out of some slasher film. There was no answer at the first door I knocked on. I don't know, maybe there was nobody home, but I could hear the TV on. Either way, I moved on to the neighbor's house in hopes of a better response. This time somebody did answer the door, a nice older woman, probably in her sixties, but her eyes got pretty damn wide when she did. For my part, I did my best to tell her the situation in a calm and soothing voice, figuring that me panicking right then probably wasn't going to help. For some reason people are kind of leery of big screaming dudes covered in blood.

To her credit, the woman, who later introduced herself as Angie, took it all in pretty good stride and retreated to go find me something for my rather obvious problem. While she was gone, I felt a little woozy, so I sat down on her stoop. She came back with some wet wipes which I pressed against my skull while she fussed and offered to take a picture of my head on her phone so I could see the damage. I accepted her offer, but the photos were pretty inconclusive given that a lot of blood was still coming out and my ability to focus wasn't quite what it had been before. On Angie's part, she admitted she was pretty far from a doctor, but she did offer to let me come inside, at least until I asked whether or not she had carpets and reminded her about the copious amounts of blood. Most of our interaction after that was mostly silence, with a few scattered remarks of sympathy by Angie here and there, until the flow out of my head became more of a seep.

When the situation improved somewhat, Angie offered to drive me to the hospital, but feeling quite a bit better, I requested a shift in destination to my house. Angie complied, though she made the offer of the hospital at least five more times in the mile it took to get me back home, heavily suggesting her opinion on the matter. Either way, when we got to my house she asked me one last time before stating that she would help me clean up more, but she was worried that she would just end up hurting me. I assured her that I had a lot of friends who were more than willing to hurt me. She then insisted on giving me her phone number, after which I thanked her and we went our separate ways.

Back in my house I retrieved my phone and started making calls. My head was still bleeding and I needed someone to help clean it out. My first thought was to call Devin, but given how things stood, I thought better of it and started with Nick and Phoebe, who after all were the closest people I knew house wise, meaning it would be less of an inconvenience for them to come over. Nick answered and I explained the situation, but upon figuring out they were in a restaurant I quickly took back my request. After all, they had just ordered drinks and it wasn't like I was dying or anything. After that the call order continued based on relative distance. My second call was to Glen, but he was just closing shop in Beaverton and wouldn't be back home for at least another forty-five minutes. I asked him if his wife Lindsey was home, which he answered in the affirmative. However, a further inquiry into how well she dealt with blood convinced me that it was probably best to move on down the list. Paul wasn't home either. The fourth time was the charm. Kevin was home and he'd be right over.

Right over turned out to be about thirty minutes, during which time I mostly scrolled through Facebook on my phone and repeatedly glanced out the window. To be honest, I didn't feel all that terrible and felt a little silly having to call somebody for help. Kevin arrived with a bottle of hydrogen peroxide and a bad attitude. Katie was with him, but she pretty much spent the whole time out in the car talking on her phone. Something about work. I'll tell you what, Kevin can be a bit of a son of a bitch, but he's got one hell of a bedside manner. I didn't think the bastard could be so gentle. He got me all cleaned up, picked a couple of pieces of tree out of my gash with a pair of tweezers, and even offered to superglue the damn thing shut if I wanted. I wasn't so sure about the last one, so after a few more pictures of my scalp and a little debate, we decided to leave it be and he went on his way.

It was at this point that I realized that I probably was going to need dinner, but that I really didn't want to make or go get anything myself. It wasn't that I probably couldn't do either of those things, even though my head was still bleeding, it was more along the lines that there are only so many instances in our lives where we get to be super pathetic, and I sure as hell wasn't going to waste this one. Now of course, you just can't be pathetic to anyone. You can only be pathetic to people who have seen you be that pathetic before. Given that I had already called most of those people, it pretty much just left me with one option. At least that's what I told myself.

Calling one's ex is never an easy thing, especially when you're feeling a little on the vulnerable side. So I texted her. I didn't know how she would react. We were well past screaming at each other, we didn't leave get togethers anymore when the other showed up, and we had even managed to have some polite small talk here and there. Overall, all things considered, things between us were about as good as they'd been in months. Probably not rush out and help me good, but hell, it was worth a shot. One can never tell with Devin, she has a pretty strong mothering instinct. Well, that instinct must have won, because not only did she text me back and agree to bring me some food, she even on her own decided to go out of her way to get it for me from my favorite Thai place.

While I was waiting, Nick texted me and let me know that they'd be stopping by on their way home to check on me. I was a little nervous about them being there at the same time as Devin, but really seeing no way out of it, I just decided to say fuck it and let things happen as they may. When Devin showed up she took one look at my head and insisted I go to the hospital. Didn't even let us have an awkward silence or anything. It didn't stop either, she kept right at it, even as she got me a fork and gave me my food. I did my best to deflect her request, but she kept pestering until finally, the both of us exasperated, I agreed to go if either Nick or Phoebe thought I should go too. The pad thai was pretty good.

When Nick and Phoebe showed up, Phoebe was drunk off her ass. It had been half price bottle of wine night down at the Montage. After examining my wound carefully, she started laughing and then went to the back of the house to use the bathroom. Nick's opinion fell strongly on the side of Devin's that I should probably go to the hospital, where they would probably give me some stitches or staples. Phoebe, re-emerging from the bathroom, stated that she would be more than glad to staple my head for me. Nick took Phoebe home. A victorious Devin took me to ZoomCare.

I don't know what it is about urgent care. You can be the only one there and they still make you wait at least fifteen minutes before they let you in. Devin spent most of the time ridiculing me for still wearing my blood covered tech shirt. What the hell did she want me to do, get another shirt bloody? At the very least the doctor was good looking. She had these beautiful green eyes. Devin of course insisted on going back with me. Beats me why the hell she felt the need to. I kind of wish she hadn't. It made flirting with the good looking doctor awkward as hell.

Anyways, the doc told me that they could just leave my head as is or they could staple it. There would be less of a scar if they stapled it, which the doctor suggested pretty heavily, given my, as she put it, hairline. Devin got a good laugh out of it. The doc had a point. I agreed and next thing you know the doctor brings out this little piece of cheap plastic and drives five staples in my head. Devin got the whole thing on video. She had it up on Facebook before we even left. When we got back into the car Devin mentioned something about how good looking the doctor had been. I agreed. Devin then pointed out the fact that the doctor had been wearing a wedding ring.

When we got home, Devin insisted on staying over since the doctor had told us that I had a mild concussion. She was all freaked out that I was going to die in my sleep or something. Christ, I tried telling her that I've had concussions before, but that didn't seem to help any. I finally just gave in. I expected her to sleep on the couch or something, but nope, pulled that shirt she sleeps in out of her car and climbed right in my bed on the side she used to always sleep on. Hell of a thing. I don't know. I was too wrecked to deal with it. I put my shirt in some warm salt water in the bathroom sink and went to bed. So anyways, there you go. That's how you get blood out of a shirt.

Just soak it overnight in some warm salt water. Works every time.

Simple Syrup

Jolene wanted pisco sours. Eddie didn't really care for pisco sours, he wasn't a big fan of raw egg whites, but that wasn't really pertinent to the situation. She had mentioned it casually, more of a statement than a request, taking a puff on her vape pen and blowing it out with a satisfied purr. Eddie had done his best to ignore her, sitting at the kitchen table, gluing together a model '75 Trans-Am, snatching the occasional snort from the tube of modeling glue.

"Did you hear me?"

Eddie thought about another snort. It would be pleasant to do a little more floating, but no, that would just be trouble later.

"Yeah, I hear you."

"Can you make me one?"

"Can't you do it yourself? I'm a little busy here."

"Eddie."

Two of Eddie's fingers had dried glue on them. Eddie rubbed the unnatural surfaces together, relishing the strange sensation. A dry chitinous shell. The victim of a science experiment gone wrong. Once a normal everyday man, now imbued with the powers of an insect. With great power comes great.....

"Eddie."

Eddie got up and looked through the bottles on top of the fridge. Most were half full or less. Jolene was a woman who enjoyed a life full of variety. Eddie rarely touched the stuff, unless Jolene insisted. Too much down with too little up, but sometimes she insisted. Certain moods gave Jolene certain preferences. Not letting her drink alone sometimes had its benefits. Sometimes. The bottle of pisco was near the back. It had been awhile since she had wanted pisco sours, since Jolene had felt the need to float down the current of memory to her younger twenties, slutting her way across South America. Cavorting with a wild abandon. Never envisioning her future a decade later, her bony ass firmly planted on the flowery couch that Eddie's mother had given them. The couch Eddie had pretended was the batmobile when he was a child. Eddie's mother had a nicer couch now. It was naugahyde. It in no way resembled the batmobile.

"Eddie."

"We have the pisco."

"What about the rest?"

Eddie looked in the cupboards and the fridge. Lemons, bitters, and eggs. The thought of the goopy texture of the raw egg white in his mouth made Eddie shudder a bit. Once Jolene got drinking pisco sours she'd start telling stories at an uncomfortable level of detail. The eggs in the cupboard made Eddie uneasy. Eggs belonged in the fridge. Jolene claimed that they didn't keep eggs in the fridge in Europe. She'd shown him a couple of articles on her phone. Eddie didn't give a damn. Eggs belonged in the fridge.

"We have everything but the simple syrup."

"Do we have sugar?"

"Yeah."

"Then make some."

Eddie drummed his fingers on the kitchen counter. He looked back at the half done Trans-Am. Agent Kurt Wilder needed his car to be done. The agents of DREAD were closing in. He had to escape with the microfiche. It was his day off. Eddie had to go back to work at the Shell station the next day. Jolene had tomorrow off. She worked four tens at the tire center. It would be nice to get the Trans-Am done.

"I don't know how."

"You just heat sugar and water. How hard can it be?"

"I don't know."

"Fuck."

It used to be when Jolene got frustrated she would at least curse under her breath. Those days were long gone.

"If you don't want to make any then go to the fucking store and buy some."

"It seems kind of a waste when it's so easy to make."

"It's like fucking two dollars Eddie."

Eddie looked at the Trans-Am model again. Agent Wilder would have to wait another day. Maybe he could evade for another twenty-four hours. Maybe not. It didn't matter. The die was cast. Eddie looked down at his pants. They were faded, but didn't have any holes. His t-shirt was also acceptable. A few stains here and there, but nothing too serious to worry about. He was just going to the store. He went into the living room and sat down on the couch to put on his shoes. Jolene was still sucking on her vape pen. The air smelled like watermelon Jolly Ranchers. The television was playing *Into the Wild* on Netflix. Agent Wilder felt betrayed. He thought he could trust her.

"Do you need me to grab anything else?"

"Grab a melon if they got any. A melon would be good for breakfast."

"What kind?"

"I don't know. Not a honeydew. I don't like honeydews."

"Me neither."

Jolene gave Eddie a sideways glance, her lips on the vape pen's tip with her cheeks sunk in. Eddie watched her, but felt like some kind of voyeur. There was a crack in the ceiling behind her. Cobwebs too. Pisco sours. She always told her stories about South America when she drank pisco sours.

"What if I just got some wine instead?"

"Eddie."

Her voice was like the snap of her fingers. Eddie rose on command and headed out the door into the bright sunshine of the balcony. Their apartment was on the second story. He should have brought sunglasses. He would look cooler in sunglasses. He wasn't going back inside. Eddie let his eyes adjust and headed down the row of doors to the stairs at the corner of the building.

The Dorsey boy was sitting on the top of the stairwell. Eddie wasn't surprised given the noises coming from the corner apartment, the landlady's apartment. The boy was ten, playing Candy Crush on an iPad, the world muted by ear buds. When he saw Eddie he scooted over a bit to let him by. Eddie stopped on the landing and looked back. The Dorsey boy didn't notice. He kept his eyes screwed to the screen on his chunky lap. Eddie went down to the parking lot. It was warm out. Not uncomfortably hot, but definitely warm. Eddie thought about Jolene's Taurus, but quickly let the idea go. She'd need the gas day after tomorrow. Eddie gave the car a last once over, waved at the two men smoking in the corner of the lot under a half dead elm, and started walking.

The moment Agent Wilder's foot landed on the cracked concrete of the sidewalk, he was forced to accept the fact that Prague wasn't what it used to be. It looked nothing like Jolene's photos, the ones she insisted on hanging in their room. Intermixed blocks of crumbling concrete and no sidewalk at all,

just dirt and gravel. Faded paint and chain link fences.
Graffiti. Old pop bottles, cigarette butts, and a pile of dog shit at
the end of one block. Weeds desperately clinging to life in every
single one of society's chinks and seams. Yes, Prague had
definitely seen better days, but then again, so had Agent Wilder.

It didn't matter. He was free now. Five years of captivity.
Five years in the jungles of a country that had seemed exotic
when he had first arrived. Five years of starvation and random
beatings. It didn't matter. He was free now. All he had to do
was avoid the agents of DREAD for another twenty-four hours.
One more day, then he could escape. It was all set up. It
wouldn't be long until he was finally home. He just needed the
damn Trans-Am to be finished. A car came cruising down the
street, an Audi, waxed and flashing in the sun. Eddie tensed.
Were they watching him? Was this going to be it? He reached
underneath his shirt to the waistband of his pants. Cool and
casual, that was the way to be, don't let them think you're
reaching for your gun. The car moved past, the driver looking
straight ahead, but a kid in the back staring at Eddie. It was him.
The one they called Little Boy. One of the most dangerous
assassins in the world. Little Boy's hands were out of sight.
Agent Wilder tightened his grip on his Beretta. Little Boy's eyes
narrowed.

Eddie's phone rang. He pulled the old flip phone out of his
pocket. It was Jolene.

"Eddie."

"Yeah."

"I want a cantaloupe."

"Okay."

"Hurry the fuck up."

"Okay."

The line went dead. Eddie put his phone back in his pocket.
It wasn't the code word he was expecting. Was the whole
mission scrapped? Agent Wilder looked for the Audi. It was

gone. What if the damn corner store didn't have cantaloupes? What the hell was he supposed to do then? Eddie sure as hell didn't want to walk clear to the WinCo. That was over a mile away. Would they even have simple syrup? For just being a corner store it had quite a variety of stuff. Eddie kicked a rock with his foot. The soccer ball went skittering out ahead. Eddie moved forward and kicked it again. Defenders moved to intercept. Eddie easily dodged around one and then another. The roar of the crowd rose to a fever pitch. Thousands of camera flashes filled the stadium. Eddie didn't let it distract him. He moved forward with purpose. None of the defenders were fast enough. It was just him and the goalie. He juked left, reared back, and kicked. The goalie dived to intercept. The rock went skittering into the street, well wide of the goal. A passing car honked its horn, the driver holding a middle finger into the air. So close, but yet so far.

Eddie ignored the car and crossed the final street to the dilapidated windowless concrete box that was the corner store, the entrance a portal of glass and metal bars. A man stood near the door wearing a hoodie despite the heat. He was a nervous looking man. An open sore graced his left cheek. His eyes were furtive, a hunted animal trapped beneath layers of trembling flesh. Eddie gave the man a wide berth when he entered the store.

The door gave off an electric ding when he opened it. The market was larger than it looked outside, with mostly snacks and packaged goods, but a small selection of fruit on one side and an impressive collection of beer and wine. Behind the counter sat the proprietor, a skinny man of South Asian origin who eyed his customers with a combination of grace and suspicion which marked the gaze of those who worked long in his profession. He smiled when Eddie entered, because Eddie was known to not be a thief, and Eddie smiled back, though neither had any idea of the other's name despite their association of many years.

Eddie went back to the small fruit section and began his hunt. The queen needed the most choice and freshest of melons, and he, her most loyal knight and retainer, must retrieve it for her. The pickings were slim, bruised apples and brown bananas, and for a moment Eddie feared that his quest would take him the distance to WinCo, but luck was with him. There, on the end, sat two sad looking cantaloupes. Eddie eyed them with the discerning air of a man who knew nothing of what made a good cantaloupe, and after a minute of hefting each individually, and giving both a light knock with his knuckles, selected the one that was the less ripe of the two. Breakfast taken care of, Eddie switched focus to the primary objective of his quest. He followed his instinct and moved amongst the shelves to the small overpriced bags of flour and sugar, but the simple syrup wasn't there. He wandered aimlessly a little more and then forced himself to accept his ignorance, going to the front to ask the proprietor for help. The little man smiled as he approached, so Eddie forced himself to smile once again too.

"Do you have simple syrup?"

The man's answer was melodious.

"Simple what?"

"Simple syrup."

"Isn't that just sugar and water?"

Eddie shifted the cantaloupe from one hand to the other.

"Yep. Do you have any?"

"Maybe with the mixers, over by the wine."

The owner pointed towards a far aisle. Eddie gestured at the counter with the cantaloupe.

"Okay if I leave this here for a sec."

The proprietor shrugged.

"Sure."

Eddie put the cantaloupe on the counter. The wine aisle was magnificent to behold. Rows of bottles, fluorescent light flashing through their red and white contents, flanked by boxes and the gallon jugs containing the lowest of the low. At the end of the aisle were the mixers. Margarita and daiquiri buckets, small bottles of bitters wrapped in paper, tomato juice for bloody marys, and rows of club soda and tonic water. Eddie leaned over to look along the bottom shelves. The door dinged as somebody came in. Much to Eddie's disappointment the store had simple syrup. A few dust covered bottles on the bottom shelf. Eddie lifted one in his hands, brushed the dust off of it, and straightened his back.

The nervous looking man from outside was inside, fidgeting and examining the bags of jerky opposite the front counter. He looked up, and for a moment he and Eddie locked eyes. It was at that moment that Eddie knew what he was going to do. It was all one fluid motion, a beautiful symphony of movement that broke all expectations given by appearance. The man spun and pulled a handgun from the pocket of his hoodie. The proprietor fell back in shock, his eyes wide, his mouth open. The robber's face was contorted with manic delight.

"Give me the cash fucker!"

Eddie dived down below the level of the shelves, the bottle of simple syrup dropping from his grasp. His heart was beating like mad. Out of sight, the proprietor was evidently too slow to follow commands.

"I said give me the fucking cash man!"

The sound of jittery hands fumbling with buttons, suddenly unsure of a task so often done on automatic. Eddie nervously rubbed together the hardened surface of the dried modeling glue on two of his fingers. With great power. No, it was crazy. The proprietor's fingers were still stumbling on the cash register buttons in their blind panic.

"Hurry up, I'm going to blast you fucker!"

The proprietor was crying, his frightened voice forced through choked sobs.

"Please. Please no. I'm trying. I'm trying."

"Hurry the fuck up!"

The wine bottle came flying over the top of the aisles. It was one of the big cheap ones. A gallon of glass and syrupy burgundy sailing across the expanse. The robber saw the glint in the corner of his eye, started to turn, and caught the bottle full in the face. Down went the robber. Down went the wine, shattering into a thousand shards and a quickly spreading red sea caught in the madness of a violent tempest. Eddie followed the bottle, a mad rush of screaming frustration. The robber was trying to rise, the gun still in his hand. Eddie's foot slammed into the man's wrist. Bones crunched. The robber screamed. The gun fell to the floor. Eddie kicked the robber in the head. Once. Twice. The robber quit moving. Eddie leaned over, picked up the gun, and deposited it on the counter in front of the shocked proprietor. Eddie's entire body was vibrating. He was nearly hyperventilating. The proprietor's mouth moved a few times in silence before words came out.

"You're a hero. You're a fucking hero."

Eddie smiled at the man. One of the most genuine smiles he'd had in years.

"Call the police."

The proprietor was still stammering.

"Hero. Thank you. Thank you."

Eddie bent forward and patted the proprietor on the shoulder.

"It's okay. Call the police. I'm going to get out of here."

Eddie scooped up the cantaloupe and headed out the door. The proprietor, face beaming, watched him go. Eddie paused for a second outside, letting his eyes adjust to the bright sunshine, and then he started back towards home. The sunshine felt good on his skin. A bird flitted from electric pole to electric pole, staying just ahead of him, pausing only here and there to let loose with a few snags of song.

The men weren't smoking under the elm anymore when Eddie got back to the apartment complex, but the Dorsey boy

189

was still sitting on the step playing Candy Crush with his chubby fingers. The raucous sounds were still emanating from the landlady's apartment. Eddie pushed his way past the boy and slammed on the corner apartment's door with the flat of his hand.

"Quit kicking your damn kid out on the step you slut!" The noises inside stopped. The Dorsey boy stood up, he looked at Eddie, confused and shocked. Eddie gave the boy a nod and headed down the balcony, whistling as he went. Eddie opened the door to the apartment he shared with Jolene. She was still sitting on the couch, puffing on her vape pen. Her eyes fell on the cantaloupe in his hand.

"You forgot the fucking simple syrup, didn't you?"

Eddie turned around without saying a word. He walked back out onto the balcony and closed the door behind him. Jolene's muffled voice was calling his name. He retreated back the way he had come. The animalistic noises were coming from the corner apartment again. The Dorsey boy was back sitting on the top of the steps. Eddie breathed in and let out a sigh. He tapped the boy lightly with his foot.

"You shouldn't have to deal with this shit. Do you want to get a pop or something?"

The boy pulled out one of his ear buds and looked at the man towering above him.

"What?"

"I said do you want to get a pop or something? You know, so you don't have to sit out here."

The boy's eyes narrowed.

"What are you, some kind of a chimo? Fuck off."

Eddie took another breath and let it out again. The Dorsey boy was staring at him with hostility. Eddie pushed past the kid and went back down the stairs. He stopped in the middle of the parking lot, alone but for the cantaloupe still in his hand. A police car glided slowly past down the street. It was getting hot out. Things were heating up. Agent Wilder ran towards the abyss as fast as his legs could carry him. With all his strength he threw the bomb in his hand out into the emptiness. It hung in the air, the timer rapidly approaching zero. The throw had been just in the nick of time. The bomb splattered itself across the asphalt of the street.

Insert Title Here

"I want to have a baby."

Jolene wasn't sure why she said it. Okay, that was a lie. She knew perfectly well why she said it. The look on Eddie's sweaty red face was priceless. There he was, giving it his all, just about to cross the finish line, and with just six words his whole world came crashing down. From the height of ecstasy to a pit of confusion and fear.

"What?"

Eddie's momentum slowed, but he was still running on fumes. Jolene gave the knife a final twist.

"I decided about a month ago."

Eddie glanced towards the dresser drawer where Jolene kept her pills, his eyes narrowing, and then looked down at her face, trying to ascertain the truth. He attempted a few more half-hearted thrusts, but he was already just pushing rope. With a disgruntled groan he pulled out of her and rolled over onto her side of the bed. They always did it on his side. She refused to sleep in the wet spot. With a self-satisfied purr Jolene rose out of the bed and put her panties back on, the fabric cutting off half the view of the flowers tattooed on each hip. Eddie lay in the bed, still breathing hard, absentmindedly playing with what remained of his chub. Without a word she turned out the light and climbed back into bed, shoving him over onto his side. Eddie rolled over dutifully and tried to put a hand on her leg, but Jolene slapped it away. She could hear him chewing on the insides of his cheeks, the sound he always made when he was uncertain.

"But we're not even married."

"We'll talk about it in the morning."

The tone was the perfect blend of sharp directness and tired indifference. Eddie didn't say another word. Jolene rolled over so that her back was to him. It wasn't that he was bad in bed, though he was far from the best. Who had been the best? That fellow backpacker in Peru? Those two guys in Chile? The dishwasher in Costa Rica? A police car went by outside, sirens blaring. Another followed a minute later. Eddie started snoring. Jolene wanted him to get one of those sleep apnea machines, but it wasn't going to happen. Just one more thing on a long list of things they both wished they had. Yes, it was Javier. Definitely Javier. The thought made her shudder. It took awhile to fall asleep.

Eddie made eggs in the morning. He was up and around before the alarm went off, which was twice as impressive considering he didn't have to go to work that day. His weekend changed all the time, but this week it was Monday and Tuesday. Jolene's always stayed the same, the weekend plus Monday, the benefit of working four tens and staying with the same job for more than a year. The smell of eggs quickly filled the little apartment, wafting across the dusty furniture and through the cobwebs in the corners. The eggs were over hard with the yolks almost chalky, a hint of salt and pepper, just the way she liked them.

"This one's kind of burned."

Eddie leaned forward to look at the egg she was poking with her fork.

"It doesn't look burnt."

"I'm not eating it."

"Whatever."

Eddie looked a little butt hurt. Jolene watched him with the practiced air of a long term observer. There was such a thing as pushing it a little too far. All in all he wasn't that bad to have around, and besides, she was pretty sure she couldn't afford to stay where they were without his income, at least for now. It was a shitty apartment, but she sure as hell could be doing worse. Eddie knew the math too, or at least she was pretty sure he did, having reminded him of it several times before, but one could never tell when the little glue sniffer might go off the rails and let his emotions get the better of him. No, sometimes it was better to add a little sugar.

"Fuck it. Waste not want not."

Jolene carved a chunk off of the offending egg and put it in her mouth. Eddie watched her chew it.

"Do you want to talk about what you said last night?"

"I have to go to work."

Jolene left her dirty dish on the table and went to the bathroom to get herself ready. Teeth, makeup, hair pulled back into a tight ponytail. The one closet in the bedroom was full of clothes, though none of them were Eddie's. His were in the dresser. You didn't need to look that nice when you worked at the gas station. Even her t-shirts were on hangers. Khakis, a white camisole, and a gray polo with her name embroidered over her heart. The Firestone logo was over the other side. The shirt was baggy on her. She left it untucked. For a moment Jolene considered taking the plastic case of her birth control pills with her, it would drive Eddie nuts, but she decided not to. Instead she grabbed her keys, phone, and vape pen and headed out the door.

It was cool outside. Wind blown dead leaves were packed under the stairwell and along the fence which lined the parking lot. Jolene started sucking on the vape pen as soon as she got outside. The canister was pineapple. Not her favorite, but it would do. Eddie didn't like it when she vaped. She didn't give a shit. She used to smoke. Vaping seemed like a good enough compromise. Jolene's Taurus sat in its space covered in dust. The transmission had gone out a week ago. They were still scraping together the funds to fix it. Jolene wanted to get a new car, but Eddie thought he could probably change out the transmission if they could get a rebuilt one. The little bastard did have clever hands.

Jolene started walking to the bus stop. Six blocks, only half of which had sidewalks. The rest were just gravel that crunched under her feet. Two men whistled at her across the street. She raised her hand in a one finger salute, but her back arched a little as she walked. She joined the small knot of people waiting for the bus, and when it arrived, took in a last few deep puffs off her vape pen and put it in her purse. The bus driver leered at her when she put her change in the slot. There weren't many seats left. One next to a bug eyed guy who looked like he was on something, one next to a hacking old crone, and one next to a fat guy who could have been the bus driver's brother, pervy stare and all. Jolene decided to stand. The plastic handle hanging from the ceiling felt sticky in her hand. The bus lurched forward, stopped as a car made a last minute dash to pass, and then lurched forward again.

Jolene watched the faces around her out of the corner of her eye, looking away if anybody looked at her. A few people talked, but most were quiet. One guy with a hardhat was listening to death metal loud enough for the whole bus to hear. Everybody looked tired, far too tired for being at the beginning of the day. The bus rattled on towards 82nd, the cityscape passing by resembling a cracked vase poorly fixed with glue. Her phone beeped. Jolene let out a sigh and dug it out of her purse.

I need you to double check the inventory as soon as you get in.

Bobby, that son of a bitch. It was supposed to be his job as manager to do inventory. Fucking Bobby. Manager extraordinaire. All powerful lord of his tiny fiefdom of tires and auto repair, the farthest west enclave and one fourth of Ronald Stuckee's empire. Jolene put her phone back into her purse, right next to the white envelope that contained her golden handcuffs. She hadn't told Eddie about it. It was really none of his damn business. A letter signed by Ronald Stuckee himself, his signature smeared by his sausage fingers. It was short and to the point. She was doing a great job and he was bumping her pay up by a dollar and a half an hour. Double digits now. Really raking in the dough. Eddie didn't need to know. It would be a nice little addition to her secret hoard. Her ace in the hole if she ever needed leverage or escape. At least it would be someday.

Bobby had the been the one to give her the letter last Friday. He had handed it over with an insincere smile on his weasely face and fatherly words of congratulations that made her want to punch him in his bespectacled nose. He'd known what it was same as her, just more proof that he wasn't going to be able to fire her any time soon. Ron liked her. She could tell. He wasn't exactly known for his generous raises. The big gorilla wasn't a bad guy. Sure he looked her up and down every time he came in, but at least he knew the difference between looking and trying something. Jesus what a compromise. At least it was better than some. The mechanics were always making comments. One had to accept such shit from mechanics, but at least they were on equal terms. There was nothing they could do if she bawled them out. Ron had walked in once when she was smearing one of their asses two ways to Sunday. He had called her spunky ever since. Ron liked backbone. Jolene's phone dinged again.

You also need to get the accounts done by noon.

Mother fucker. She could see Bobby sitting behind his desk in what had once been the utility closet back by the tires, straightening the flopped over monstrosity he referred to as his executive haircut. Leering at her when he called her in. Telling her to close the door. She never closed the god damn door. Some mistakes you only make once. It wasn't even her fucking job. All she was supposed to do was answer the phone, schedule drop offs, and collect the money. It was supposed to be his job to balance the accounts and do the fucking inventory. It was why he made twice as much as her. A bunch of bullshit, that was what it was. She did all the work. He got all the credit, but what was she going to do? Ron liked Bobby. The little twerp had put in his time. Good old boys like Ron might like backbone, but they liked loyalty even more. They put great stock in the chain of command.

Jolene had often thought of fucking Bobby over, but what then? Bobby couldn't fire her, but he sure as hell could make her life a living hell. Any sign of rebellion was to be quickly quashed. Cut back hours, refusals of days off, a long list of mundane and mind numbing tasks. Bobby knew his tools well and handled them with the adeptness of a master. If she complained it would always be the same.

"You know, we really need you to be a team player. We all got to help each other out to get ahead."

He always leered at her tits when he said it. Sometimes he would try giving her the eye. It always made her want to puke. Sometimes she wished the little fucker would actually try something, she knew the law, she'd read up on that shit, but the little fucker was too smart for that. If she kept complaining the second catchphrase would make an appearance.

"You can always get another job."

Sure fucker. Easy peesey. Just get another job. Just throw away three years of raises and seniority. Maybe she could just go work for minimum wage at the gas station with Eddie, back to how it used to be when she met him. Fuck that. Her phone dinged again. It was Eddie this time.

I want to talk about what you said last night when you get home.

A second ding.

I hope you have a good day :)

Fuck all of it. The bus came to a halt at her stop on 82nd. People filed off and on. The bus driver looked at her in his mirror expectantly, then shrugged his shoulders and shut the door. The bus ground back into gear, turned up 82nd and around the block, and then began its descent back into the wilds. Jolene got off at the next stop and pulled out her vape pen. The bus drove away. The bench at the stop had an advertisement on it telling her to visit Nebraska. Sure, fucking Nebraska. Come see our big rocks that kind of look like things. A car sped past and honked its horn. Jolene ignored it, still laughing to herself about Nebraska. She reached into her purse for her phone. Fuck all of it.

Can't make it in today. Got the flu.

She waited for the ding.

How bad?

Fuck him.

Bad enough not to come into work.

You don't have any more sick days. You won't get paid.

Fine.

Okay.

Bobby always had to get the last word. Jolene was unsure what to do now? She sure as hell couldn't go back home. Eddie would be there and she didn't feel like dealing with him. Jolene shivered. It wasn't all too warm outside and dark clouds were on the horizon. It was probably going to rain soon. She started walking towards the nearest Max station, puffing her vape pen as she went.

It was less cold at the station, nestled in the artificial dry riverbed of the freeway it was sheltered from the wind. A plethora of working stiffs waited with her. When the commuter train arrived ten minutes later it was already crowded with those from further up the line. Jolene didn't buy a ticket, but she filed on with all the rest. She worked her way up the aisle until the cram from the door on the other end of the car stopped her cold. She was wedged between some kid in baggy pants and a guy in a polo shirt like hers, just a different logo. The train lurched into motion and she was on her way.

Everyone was silent as they rode, lost in their own little worlds. Jolene wasn't tall enough to see much around her, just a press of shirts, jackets, and blouses. A colorful forest biome with her in the shade of the those better designed to thrust themselves upward into the sunlight. Alone, but for the occasional glance of eyes tracking their way aimlessly through the wilderness. At each stop more pressed their way on, the acceptable area of personal space shrinking with each shuddering halt of the Max. Somebody let out a stifled curse over a tread on foot. The man in the polo pressed against her so tight that she could feel the pressure against her breasts. He mumbled an apology and then looked away, embarrassed by his inability to separate himself from her. Jolene didn't say anything, but the moment the shuffling mass provided a reprieve she shoved her purse between them. The man looked grateful.

There were transit officers at the Gateway station. As the doors opened they filed on in pairs, ready to start checking tickets as soon as the doors closed. The last thing Jolene needed was a fine. She joined those filing out, slipping her way out of the tightening noose around her neck. It didn't matter. Three lines joined at Gateway before making their way to downtown. The Green from the south, the Blue from the east, and the Red from the north. Her Green train pulled away. A Blue pulled in less than three minutes later. It was just as packed. Jolene shoved her way aboard. The Max train started moving. Somebody let out a loose phlegmy cough. The pack of humanity shifted as those closest tried to move away, momentarily clearing Jolene's view of the window. Countless cars sat on the freeway, inching their way forward towards downtown, but racing forward at sixty-five in the opposite direction. The Max stopped at the next station, more people filed aboard, and the view was gone.

The closer the Max got to downtown the more the crowd changed. Minorities and working class filtered out, replaced by hipsters, business casual, and the never ending sea of polos worn by those in the service industries. Jolene didn't look out of place. A handsome man in a suit gave her the once over. Jolene jutted out her chest to give him a better view. He looked away. His was a different station. The train rumbled over the Steel Bridge and into downtown, its pace slowed by the numerous close together stops. Old Town. Skidmore Fountain. Pioneer Place. The flow of people reversed with more getting off then on. Galleria. Providence Park. Kings Hill almost immediately after so the rich people at the athletic club wouldn't have to walk the block to Providence Park. Jolene took a seat. The car was almost empty. At Goose Hollow two middle aged men in tights got on with bikes. One hung his up on the rack by the door while the other held his protectively close, wary of anything that might cause the slightest scratch. One gestured towards the other's contraption.

"Are those the new road wheels?"

"Yeah, Zipp 30's."

"How much?"

"I got a deal. Only five hundred a piece."

"Nice."

Jolene could see the shape of their dicks against the fabric of their biking shorts. The Max trundled into the tunnel and left downtown behind. At the Zoo stop the two bikers got off to ride the elevator to the top of the hill. The train moved on, exiting back into the sunlight next to another freeway, a mirror image of the one before. Everyone had a seat now with room to spare. People got on and off in singles or pairs instead of bunches. Jolene got out her vape pen and took a couple of puffs, filling the air with the scent of artificial pineapple. Nobody said anything. Apartments, houses, and strip malls dotted the landscape around her. Outside of the freeway everything looked quiet and peaceful.

When the Max reached the end of the line in Hillsboro, Jolene stayed aboard and rode it back towards downtown. The train only stopped long enough for the driver to get out to pee. The landscape slid past in reverse, the only difference being the freeway being more clear than it had been before. Two women got on the train at the first stop. They sat together and talked quietly in Spanish. Everyday minutiae mostly, with a smattering of gossip thrown in. Jolene laid her head against the cool glass and with the quiet Spanish in her ear watched the world pass by.

They'd gone down the summer of her junior year. Katie with money given to her by her grandmother and Jolene with savings from a job and a federally subsidized loan meant to be used on tuition and board. Chile had been the destination, due to its wide variety of climates, closeness to the Andes, and the insistence of Katie's father that it was the only Latin American country where one could trust the police. Santiago, Valparaiso, Pucon, and San Pedro de Atacama, just to name a few. Three months of exotic grand adventure with all of their lives contained in two backpacks. At the end Katie returned home, but Jolene fell in with a group heading north into Peru. She hadn't wanted the adventure to end. She had tasted freedom and she would be damned if she returned to a world of expectations.

The group's plan was to work its way up the Pacific coast all the way to Vancouver. No plans and no timeline, just an idea of a destination. They stayed in hostels and cheap motels, even at times sleeping in parks under the stars. They pooled money they earned doing odd jobs and stretched their budget by dumpster diving. They travelled via train and bus, though as time went on hitchhiking became more the norm. They partied often, sampling anything they could get their hands on, leading to the expected good times and bad. On several occasions she woke up as part of a naked pile. It took them over two years to work their way north through Peru, six months of which were just spent in Mancora. It was the best of times. Katie visited Jolene there after she graduated with a degree in marketing, but though willing to partake in the life again, it gained no permanent foothold.

Only a few of the original group were still together by the time they reached Ecuador. Arguments, distractions, and memories of home all took their toll. New people joined here and there, but none seemed to last very long. By the time they reached Panama City, five years into the journey, Jolene had been the only one left. Everyone else had dropped away. It hadn't mattered. There was still places to see and one could always find the right kind of people if one knew where to look. It had all ended in Costa Rica, not long after her 26th birthday. The goal was abandoned in light of the needed procedure, which even in the most backwards parts of the country, was still safer to get in the States than Costa Rica. Of course there were costs to coming home, three years of college debt and claims of subsidized loan fraud just to name a few. In a brave new world where degrees were a dime a dozen, it wasn't an auspicious start.

The two women speaking Spanish got off at the Sunset Transit Center, leaving Jolene the solitary occupant of the car. Alone she entered the tunnel that exited into downtown. It was almost noon. Maybe she should give Katie a call, or just send her a text, see if she wanted to meet up for lunch. Katie worked downtown for a property management firm. She lived downtown too, in a cute little apartment just off Burnside. One of the old ones that looked the same as it had in the 1950's. Katie seemed to be doing okay for herself, or least at least that's what her Facebook pictures suggested. Lots of photos of rock climbing and evening dresses on rooftop bars with a handsome man on her arm with spiked hair. They hadn't spoken in over a year. It would be nice to see her. There was no animosity. They had simply drifted apart the inhabitants of two different worlds. The Max came to a stop at Pioneer Square. Jolene got out. Her phone stayed in her purse.

The streets were filled with moving people. Thousands of ants emerging from their holes to feed over the lunch hour, mixing in with the small packs of tourists, random delivery drivers, and hustling people who seemed to believe that a timely arrival at their destination was of the greatest importance. The homeless took it all in from their perches against walls and on street corners, watching the world pass them by with hungry eyes and outstretched fingers. She walked the streets for awhile, trying to decide whether or not to try to get a hold of Katie until the time made such musings moot. Hungry, she went into the nearest pub to find a bite to eat.

It was a fancy place. Big wooden bar and backdrop filled with liquor bottles up to the ceiling, the highest of which was only reachable via a sliding ladder. A woman in a black dress moved amongst the tables and booths, watching over the last portions of the lunch crowd. The bartender wore a vest and tie. He was a handsome guy in his late twenties. Jolene chose to sit at the bar. The bartender sauntered over, his manner easy,

displaying that he knew what he had to offer. He smiled
politely, though a little forced, and Jolene smiled back. The
bartender put a hand on the bar.

"Need anything?"

"Do you have any pisco?"

"No."

"What do you have on draft?"

The bartender took in a short breath and let it out, then
gestured towards the taps behind him. Jolene looked over his
shoulder.

"I'll have the Drifter and a menu."

The bartender nodded, slid over a menu from a nearby pile,
and went to get her drink. Everything in the menu looked over
priced. With the exception of some appetizers, nothing was
under twenty bucks. The bartender came back with her beer.

"Have you decided on something?"

"I'll take the mimosa salad with shrimp."

"Of course."

The bartender moved down the bar to put in her order and
then stayed at the other end to talk to the waitress. They
conversed quietly together, glanced in Jolene's direction,
conversed again, and then laughed. Jolene eyed the liquor
bottles on the shelves in front of her. She wondered how much
the most expensive one was. When her food came out the
bartender brought it to her, but left again soon after to serve a
well dressed couple further down before going back to chatting
with the waitress. The salad was delicious. She could feel the
bartender and waitress watching her. The waitress went into the
back. The bartender went to serve the well dressed couple again.
Jolene ran towards the exit. She heard a startled yelp as she hit
the door. She turned the corner and broke into a sprint. People
looked up, but nobody really paid her any mind. She turned a
corner again and slowed to a quick walk. Her hands pulled the
ponytail out of her hair. She crossed the street, went down a

block, and turned another corner. Her pace slowed to a sedate pace. Nobody was after her. Most people who make the majority of their money off of tips will only try so hard. Jolene was laughing with giddy excitement. It was just like old times.

She was still laughing fifteen minutes later. Jolene wandered the streets with no destination in mind. Sometimes a store would catch her eye so she'd go in to browse, no intention of buying. The stationary store, a furniture store, and a nice boutique dress place. A few city workers, lounging around an open manhole, gave her the up and down as she passed. A few blocks later a homeless looking gentleman came down the street, shrieking at everybody and nobody.

"It's no secret. It's no secret people."

Several people turned around or crossed over to the other side of the street. Jolene kept going forward. The crazy man eyed her as the distance between them closed. His peepers rolled in his head and then focused on her with a strange intensity, his whole body leaning forward. He chewed on his lips and his fingers played an imaginary piano. Jolene's muscles tensed. The man's face contorted into a terrifying mask.

"Niggers!"

Jolene jumped. The man kept moving down the street, laughing as he went. By the time he reached the other end of the block he was already back to his original rant.

"It's no fucking secret. No fucking secret."

She wandered on. Sunlight filtered through the canyons of concrete and steel, flashing off of modern monstrosities of glass, illuminating brick edifices from another world. The homeless were everywhere. Young and old. Sitting and wandering. Some asking for change, some sitting in silence, and a few even playing old instruments of one kind or another. At one corner a man beat the bottoms of plastic buckets with drumsticks in a quick rhythmic pattern that made her want to dance. She stood and watched him for a while, studying his

206

smiling visage as the upturned cap in front of him filled with coins and dollar bills. Jolene added a few dollars of her own before moving on.

Jolene puffed on her vape pen as she walked, exuding a cloud of pineapple fragrance as she went. She went into more stores, but mostly to escape from the cold to the warmth inside. One store sold nothing but different vinegars, its interior a maze of glass carboys filled with liquid ranging from clear to the darkest night. Silver spouts stood at attention on the front of each, awaiting their turn to provide. A bell above the door rang when she entered, and it rang again when she left soon after catching the proprietor staring at her ass.

In some of the stores they watched her in a different way, eying her as she moved amongst the wares, standing out due to her plumage. The vintage stores weren't so bad. The hipsters behind the counters watched all with disinterest edged slightly by a contempt broadcasted at all equally. The boutique stores were another matter. Immaculately dressed women with straight postures and coiffed hair casually followed her around the store, smiling so sweetly when Jolene turned to look back at them.

"Do you need any help finding anything?"

"No just browsing."

"All right, well, just let me know if you need any help."

They'd stand there, smiling like idiots, waiting for Jolene to move away, and once she reached the prescribed distance, following again and watchig her every move. It was maddening. So maddening that Jolene finally broke down and purchased a hundred and eighty dollar turtleneck. The woman behind the counter smiled as though Jolene was a long lost cousin when she rang it up.

"What a beautiful turtleneck. I hope you enjoy it."

"Yeah, it's very soft."

"It's merino wool. Would you like a bag?"

"Thank you."

Two blocks down the street the bag ended up in a garbage can in the ladies room of dark bar still waiting for the end of the work day to truly kick off happy hour. In a dirty stall, Jolene took off her polo, carefully folding it before shoving it into her purse. The bra beneath was frayed and faded, but such things became invisible when she pulled the soft fabric of the green turtleneck down over her head. When she walked back out of the ladies room the bartender gave her an up and down. Jolene thought about having a drink, but instead headed straight out the door back into the sunlight. From that point on the women at the boutique stores were more genuinely friendly.

It felt strange to be wandering the streets in the middle of the afternoon. She wasn't supposed to be there. Part of her felt like an imposter. A spy from another kingdom, cleverly disguised to root out the secrets of a world where the numbered streets were in the single digits. When she grew tired of the boutique stores she went into the Pioneer Place mall. In the Nordstroms, an exasperated young clerk bit her lip in frustration as a finely dressed middle aged man forced upon her the unwanted task of measuring his inseam to make sure it hadn't miraculously changed since the last time he'd purchased pants. At the bookstore a middle aged woman in the literary classics section seductively eyed a young adonis leafing through a copy of *Wuthering Heights*, unaware of the woman old enough to be his mother entwining him in secret fantasies. Back out on the street a girl in her late teens stopped Jolene with a compliment as she moved past.

"I really like your shirt."

The girl was quiet as a mouse, so quiet that Jolene almost didn't hear her. The girl wore baggy jeans made for men, filthy from lack of washing. Her ratty hair exploded in greasy curls out from underneath a grungy ballcap shoved tightly on her head. A chipped and worn skateboard was held under one arm. Jolene arrested her forward movement, turning to eye the girl who looked away in nervous shame for speaking up. Jolene smiled to let the girl know that it was okay.

"Thank you."

The girl nodded in a jerky fashion and turned away to continue her way down the street. A big dog sitting between two homeless men lunged at her with sudden ferocity, snarling and baring its teeth. The girl fell back against a newspaper box, shrinking into herself as she cowered against the yellow metal. The man holding the dog's leash barked at her just as ferociously as his charge.

"He doesn't like fucking skateboarders."

The girl's voice barely emerged from her throat, a mumble choked by horrified fear at her own transgression of daring to walk down the street.

"I'm sorry. I'm sorry."

The man would have none of it. There was no sympathy in his eyes.

"Just get the fuck out of here."

The girl retreated, nearly running in her haste to escape the confrontation. Jolene was on them in an instant.

"Leave her the fuck alone."

Her heart was pounding in her chest. The dog was between Jolene and the men, growling and snapping. The owner fell back in surprise, recovered, and threw himself back into the fray.

"What the fuck business is it of yours?"

The girl was running now, pushing herself as fast as she could to fully escape. The owner was red in the face. His comrade was laughing, uncontrollable guffaws which echoed off the building walls. People were watching, but Jolene didn't care. She could feel the heat rising from her body, frizzing her hair with its rage.

"Control your fucking dog."

"Don't tell me how to handle my dog you fucking bitch."

"Fuck off you piece of......"

It hit her squarely in the stomach. Half an eaten
cheeseburger lofted by the hand of the compatriot. It seemed to
stick there for a moment before falling, leaving behind smears of
mustard and ketchup. Jolene looked down in horror at the
yellow and red upon the green. The owner was laughing with
his companion. Jolene's fists were clenched. People stood
watching from a distance, entranced by the drama playing before
their eyes. The girl was gone. Jolene could feel hot tears
threatening to overwhelm her. The dog fell into a quizzical
silence. The two men couldn't stop laughing. She saw herself
kicking and hitting them. Pounding their heads into the
sidewalk. It all came out in a primal scream.

"Fuck you."

Jolene turned and marched away, spine straight, refusing to
look back lest the two men see the tears flowing down her face.
People moved out of her way. She ducked into the first bar that
she came to. It was the same bar where she had changed into the
turtleneck. It was empty except for the bartender, whose pale
face followed her as she rushed past to the seclusion of the ladies
room. Once safely ensconced she let the tears fall as they would.
She stood by the sink, her callused hands desperately attempting
to fix what had befallen via the double assault of water and paper
towels. It did little to help. The offending sauces were easy
enough to remove, but the stains clung on with a tenacity which
set her teeth on edge. At last, abandoning hope, she hid herself
in a stall to give time for both her eyes and turtleneck to dry.

The bar was starting to fill when Jolene emerged from the
bathroom. The pale bartender was working quickly, filling beers
and throwing bullshit at the regulars. They came filing out of
office buildings down into the watering holes. There were a few
button down shirts here and there, but most of the crowd were
young men and women dressed casually in fashions that
suggested good paying jobs with loose dress codes. They
clinked glasses together, bludgeoning the shy with verbal

insistence that eye contact must be maintained throughout the ritual. They talked above each other and laughed with wild abandon which filled the bar with a half mad glee from re-achieving their freedom once again. Jolene, preferring to stay near the outskirts of the revelry, found herself a seat at the far end of the bar. She caught the pale bartender's eye, but even then it was at least five minutes before he was able to make his way down to her.

"What will you have?"

"Can you make a pisco sour?"

"A what?"

"A Ranier will be fine."

The pale bartender moved away and then came back with her drink. He set it down and gave her an appraising look, taking in the puffiness of her cheeks and the blots of discoloration on the green of her top.

"Is that wool?"

"Yeah, merino."

"Club soda will help take that out."

"I know."

"Soak it overnight."

"How much do I owe you for the beer?"

"First one's on the house. Looks like you've had the kind of day where you could use it."

Jolene looked down at the few bubbles struggling to survive together on the top of her beer. She didn't want to look the pale bartender in the eye.

"Thank you."

The bartender moved away, diving back into the rising tide of customers. Jolene drank her beer in silence, watching the undulating mass before her. Very few made it as high up the beach as she sat, and those that did were lonely creatures, out of place compared to the statistical average. When her beer was empty the bartender replaced it with another, though this time in exchange for three dollars. Her phone dinged so she got it out of her purse. It was Eddie.

When do you think you're going to make it home?

She put her phone down on the bar and went back to her beer. After about fifteen minutes the phone dinged again.

I just want to have an idea of when to get dinner ready.

Jolene turned her phone off, put it back in her purse, and ordered another beer.

The crowd was mostly gone by seven, heading home or off to other haunts. The last few dregs hung on until about eight-thirty, but in the end even they were enticed by the horrid sirens call of another coming workday. The pale bartender rubbed down the bar with his towel and then flipped it onto his shoulder before walking towards Jolene. She almost laughed at his choreographed movements, his need to know she was watching while never looking directly her way. He wasn't a bad looking guy with his dark hair and trimmed goatee. The rest looked as though it came from a package labeled devil may care, but such things were expected from those in their mid-twenties. They were still malleable and trying to find their way. He kind of reminded her of Javier in that way. He smiled as he started his approach. It was a nice smile.

"Do you need another drink?"

Jolene already had five beers sloshing in her belly and a nice sustainable buzz that would likely carry her through the night, but what the hell, there was nothing wrong with seeing where the world carried you.

"Sure."

The pale bartender moved away and Jolene watched his ass in his skinny jeans, averting her eyes to the window when he returned. The beer was not as good as the previous ones, but she sipped from it anyway, not wanting to let it go to waste. The bartender smiled.

"Not too many people stay in this place after eight, especially on a Tuesday."

Jolene sipped, looking up at him through her lashes.

"I don't mind the quiet."

The bartender stuck out his hand.

"I'm Wade. What's your name?"

"Violet."

His hand was dry and smelled of bleach, but the grip was tight in a way that conveyed strength while still being gentle. He didn't release right away, instead studying her fingers with the eyes of an art connoisseur.

"Like the character from the Willy Wonka book?"

"Something like that."

She pulled her hand back, though for a second she thought he might not let go. He smiled at her again.

"You from here, or just visiting?"

"Oh, I was born here, but just visiting right now. I do a lot of travelling."

"Yeah, where to?"

"Latin America mostly. You name a country down there and I've probably been to it."

"Suriname?"

"Of course you'd name the one I haven't been to."

They both laughed. He had a nice laugh. Kind of quiet and deep down in his chest. A rolling gentle wave of mirth.

"You been traveling long?"

"Years. Pretty much since college."

"Sounds nice."

"It's got its moments."

She sipped again from her beer. He was leaning against the bar, watching her with kind eyes with just a hint of jealousy.

"I've always wanted to travel. Maybe after I graduate."

"What are you studying."

"I'm trying to get my MBA."

"What, you don't always want to be a bartender?"

Wade laughed again. Jolene definitely liked his laugh.

"Nah, I might aim just a little higher."

"Going to be a rich man someday?"

"Maybe not rich, but maybe a little extra over starving."

"Nothing wrong with that."

They lapsed into silence. Jolene took another drink of her beer. He reminded her so much of Javier. They looked nothing alike, but the similarity was there. The same thought out movements, the same cockiness of a man with a simple dream, an attainable dream. Wade leaned over the bar towards her.

"I've always wanted to go to Peru."

"You going to take a selfie at Machu Picchu for your Tinder profile?"

"Maybe, but I'd really like to check out Mancora. I've heard a lot of good things."

Jolene flashed a smile.

"It's pretty great."

Wade was saying something, but she wasn't listening. She was seeing herself on the beach again, dancing naked beneath the stars to drumming and the bass beat of the surf. They were all around her, dancing and naked as well, those children of a lost world, howling upwards, silvery sprites in the moonlight. Wade appeared before her, still pale despite the earlier heat of the equatorial sun. His arms embraced her. His mouth found hers. No, it wasn't Wade. It wasn't the pale facsimile. It was Javier. The beach where neither man had actually ever been was gone. They were tangled in sweaty sheets in his apartment in San Jose. He was taking her like he had done before. Tearing all self-control from her corporeal form. Her voice begging him to stop, pleading that she could not take any more, while the rest of her disagreed. The rest of her demanded more until she was nothing but a cloud floating high above the world below. They lay in the darkness, fingertip sized bruises on his arms and bite

214

marks on her shoulders. He caressed her hair and cooed so sweetly. He promised to help find her a job so she wouldn't have to go. He worked in a cafe. He wouldn't work there forever, but it was something for now, a stepping stone. They needed a dishwasher. He could probably get her hired. Wade was moving away. Jolene jerked itself back into the quiet bar.

"What was that?"

"I said I need to start the dishwasher."

Jolene shuddered. Wade locked the dishwasher closed and started it humming with the push of a few buttons. He came back. Jolene's beer was half gone, but the remainder was going flat. Wade pulled a jacket out from underneath the bar.

"I need a smoke. You want one?"

Her joints stiffened. Jolene hadn't smoked since she had started dating Eddie. He claimed it bothered his sinuses. Little glue sniffer. The vape pen was a good substitute, but sometimes one needed the real thing.

"Sure."

Wade hopped over the bar in a fluid motion and then led her out the front door into the darkness. It was getting cold outside. He offered her his jacket, but she declined so he put it on himself. From the jacket pocket came a box of American Spirits. He offered her one and then took one for himself. It felt funny to be holding it between her fingers. She gestured with it and gave him a smile.

"Got a light."

He smiled back. A hungry smile.

"You bet I do."

He was on her in an instant, his cigarette forgotten on the concrete below. One arm encircled her back while the other hand squeezed her ass. His tongue was in her mouth, wet and probing. She never dropped her cigarette. She pushed with all her might. She rocked him back on his heels and spun his head with a hard slap on his cheek. His head came back around, his

eyes filled with shock and confusion. She slapped him again and
started to run. He was yelling something, but she didn't listen.
She just ran as hard as she could until she couldn't run any
more. The few people on the street watched her as she ran past,
but not one raised their hand or voice with query. There weren't
many cars on the street, but one honked when she dashed out in
front of it, though it was still half a block away.

She stopped running after about four turns and eight blocks.
She leaned against a brick wall, breathing hard. The cigarette
was still in her hand. She dropped it in her purse and picked up
her phone, but then dropped it as well. She took a hair tie out
instead and pulled her hair back into a severe ponytail. The ugly
stain on her turtleneck stared up at her. It was cold. Too damn
cold to just be standing still. She started walking, not really sure
where she was going. It had to be close to ten. There was hardly
anybody out. Just a few couples moving arm in arm and the
occasional loner with their hands deeply embedded in their
pockets.

One figure seemed to be following her. At first she thought
it must be Wade, but a quick look back proved it not to be the
case. He was a bearded man with glasses. Bigger than Wade
with the start of a paunch. He stayed about half a block behind,
their paces in unison. When he turned the same way as her the
first time she told herself it was nothing. When they shared the
same direction a second time the logical part of her brain called
it coincidence. Her lizard brain wasn't so sure. The primitive
center of her emotions screamed in warning that something was
wrong, flooding her system with adrenaline which burst forth in
a cold sweat that set her to shaking uncontrollably. She didn't
want to be out there. She just wanted to be home. She turned a
third corner. The man turned as well. Jolene dug her hand into
her purse, pulling out her phone. It was still turned off, but she
fumbled with the screen as though it could still provide
salvation. She made her fourth turn. She moved down the

sidewalk, glancing behind her as she went. The man emerged from behind the building. He was whistling to himself as he moved. He did not turn. He crossed the street and was gone, the soft pitch of his half remembered tune fading with his exit.

The adrenaline dumped her like a ton of bricks. Jolene was tired. She just wanted to go home. At the next intersection she looked at the street sign. Christ, she was clear up on Marshall and Tenth. She turned back on her phone, stomping her feet to stay warm while she waited for it to boot. There were ten text messages from Eddie, two missed calls, and one voicemail. Jolene ignored them all. She looked up the bus schedule. All she had to do was walk across the Broadway Bridge and then down to the Rose Quarter Transit Center. A direct bus would be climbing back up into the hundreds at 10:39.

The red arch of the Broadway Bridge climbed upwards into the night, curving its way over first the lit streets and then the dark river far below. It was cold out in the middle of the bridge where the span peaked before declining back down to the world below, but Jolene stopped anyways. The river moved silently, keeping its secrets to itself. To her left the lights of downtown twinkled, false stars unable to replace the ones above which lay hidden by the united forces of the artificial illumination. To her right blinked the red lights of cranes, sleeping skeletons waiting for morning to renew their efforts. Farther still was the endless sea of fallen stars upon the rolling ground, stretching to the horizon where they met the few muted fellows who still managed to hang desperately on in the heavens. Jolene stood for a moment and watched it all, tightly gripping the cold painted metal of the handrail.

The metal grew warm beneath her touch. His hands came down on either side of her. She could feel him pressed up against her. They were alone. Everyone else was gone. She could feel the heat of his breath. His rising excitement. His hands, his once gentle hands, clawed at her, tearing at her. She tried to playfully slap him away. No, not here you silly fool. Wait until later. He would not listen. The hands became stronger. She tried to push him away, but he would have none of it. He threw her down with a sudden viciousness that she had not known he possessed, pushing her head down onto the stainless steel still coated with grease and a few pieces of errant food. The dishwasher hummed to itself, contentedly cleaning the last load of the night. She begged him. She pleaded with him to stop. This was not the begging to which he had grown accustomed. No, this desperation included the overwhelming stink of fear. She tried to squirm away, but couldn't. He was too strong. There was no stopping him. He did as he wanted, and then kissed her on the back of the neck the same as he had done so sweetly so many times before.

The river flowed past down below. Jolene cried. She cried until the whole world seemed immersed in a raging sea. She had loved him. She had fucking loved him. She shuddered. Her whole body shuddered until the only thing keeping her up was her iron grip on the handrail. The shuddering slowed and then fell still. The world of false stars shimmered before her. Jolene reached into her purse and pulled out the lonely cigarette. She put it in her mouth, tasting the filter and half remembering what the world had once been. She reached into her purse again. There was no lighter. Of course there was no fucking lighter. She took the cigarette out of her mouth and held it in her hand. She stared at it a moment, taking in every detail, and then let it drop. It floated downwards on the breeze. She could feel herself following it. Down. Down. Into the river with a heavy splash. A freezing blanket enveloping her. Cooing to her as it numbed away all feeling until there was nothing left. All of it disappearing. The memories going last. Screaming out one last time until they too vanished. The cigarette floated on the water. Bobbing with every little undulation. It sat there, staring back up at her, until it was pulled out of sight under the bridge, carried by the current.

The bus was ten minutes late. Jolene paid her money and joined the few denizens returning to the high numbered wilds that were their portion of the world. She stared out the window as they travelled, watching the veneer strip away until what was left was faded, dingy, and scratched. It only took about an hour to get home. Tomorrow would be a busy day. Undoubtedly Bobby had failed to get done either the accounts or the inventory. Her escape was likely only a temporary reprieve. The walk between the bus stop and the apartment was not a long one. She was careful to watch her step. Few street lights illuminated the broken debris that could once have been called sidewalks.

The apartment was dark when she got there. Eddie was already in bed, snoring softly. Jolene didn't wake him. She brushed her teeth and undressed in the dark, hiding the stained turtleneck at the bottom of her hamper. Eddie wasn't allowed to wash her clothes. The little shit couldn't understand anything beyond the cold setting. Eddie rolled over and smacked his lips when she climbed into bed next to him. The change in position intensified his snoring. Jolene lay in the darkness, listening to the guttural growl. She wished he was awake. She wished he would try something so she could tell him no.

Scammer

hello

It was obvious that it was a scammer the moment Kevin looked at the sender's Facebook profile. Everything about it raised up red flags. Tracy Windy. From Los Angeles, California. Lives in California City, California. The profile only had eight photos, all posted in the last two weeks. Jet black hair, big brown eyes, a physique best described as curvy, not in a bad way, just a little extra to help make everything really pop. A series of small tattoo birds took flight high over the creamy white skin of her left breast. She was older, crows feet around her eyes and soft lines around her mouth, but not unattractive. Maybe early forties. She wore light pink lipstick and her eyebrows were tweezed to the point where they looked painted on. Her profile picture showed an ample amount of cleavage. In four of the pictures she was in workout clothes, sports bra and spandex tight over her ass, a flat belly in between. One picture was with an older woman, who based on the resemblance was likely her mother. Another was of her with a small boy, maybe age four or so, with matching eyes. The last picture was of baked chicken with basil leaves and a side of potatoes.

Tracy Windy only had five friends, all men. Three were older men, a laboratory worker from Japan, a redneck looking parts store worker from Florida, and a black preacher from Georgia. The other two were younger. One a young hispanic working at a sex store in Phoenix, and the other just an extremely handsome man named Sal with no other information. She was part of only two groups. Cars For Sale SA was exactly what it seemed to be, a group where people put up cars they were trying to sell in South Africa. The other was called NSFAS updates. A quick Google search showed it was the National Student Financial Aid Scheme, also in South Africa. It was so bad it was almost funny.

The only thing that gave Kevin pause was that the message wasn't to his profile. No, it was to his Facebook page, *Professor Errare Presents*, posts about random people from history who had led ridiculous lives. While the hell would a scammer send a message there? It didn't make a lot of sense. Just a few days before one of his posts had been shared by some guy in his early twenties in Birmingham, England. Anything could be possible. What could it hurt to message back.

Hello.

Kevin felt silly the moment he sent it. He wasn't sure why he even bothered to do it. Maybe he was bored. It didn't take her long to respond.

how are you doing there I saw your your profile here it was fine I will like to know you If you don't mind

Kevin felt slightly more ridiculous. Jesus Christ, they were so obviously a scammer. The least they could do is have a little professional pride. What kind of idiot fell for such shit? It was time to cut old Tracy Windy loose, let them know he was in on the trick. He didn't have time for such horseshit. He was running late.

Bwahahahahaha.

Kevin closed out of Messenger and opened Lyft. It was opening day, first Timbers match of the season and a Friday evening to boot. He was going to drink a few too many. He had earned some unwind time. It had been one hell of a week at work. The car arrived five minutes later. Kevin rushed about to make sure he had everything he needed. Scarf, tickets, money. The driver was a middle aged Russian man who only spoke a little English. The Russian was a friendly guy, excitedly sharing his taste in music, which was mostly Russian elevator music and some pretty good blues, which according to the Russian was sung by four old blind men. The Russian felt the need to inform Kevin that the blind men were all black, which was why their voices carried such resonance. Kevin politely listened for awhile, but after a bit got bored and reopened Messenger. Tracy Windy hadn't taken the hint.

how are you doing there

Persistent little bastard. For whatever reason, Kevin imagined the person on the other end was probably a guy. He looked at Tracy Windy's profile again. They were attractive pictures, probably scraped from some actual person's profile. Kevin laughed quietly to himself. Fuck the person on other end. Bunch of crooks. Might as well fuck with them back.

Pretty good. You?

where are you from

Everything on Kevin's profile was set to be hidden from anyone except his friend's list. It was just common sense. He could say anything he wanted.

Vermont.

Vermont seemed like a funny state to be from. Nothing but maple syrup and marble. The Lyft driver pulled up in front of Tony's Tavern. Kevin got out. The Russian called after him in his broken English.

"I get five star, yes?"

Kevin gave the man a thumbs up, shut the car door, and headed inside. Tony's was a dive bar, one of the few last real ones in downtown. Old usuals sat on stools they had claimed years ago, sipping cheap beer bought with social security checks. The floor was painted plywood and the booths were the same only with a thick layer of varnish instead of paint. It wasn't much to look at, but the hipsters hadn't found it yet, so it made for a good meetup point before a match. Leo and Paul were sitting in one of the booths, opened Rainier tall boys in front of them. Paul waved and Kevin walked over and sat down. They'd probably be leaving soon. No time for a beer. The three men traded greetings. *The Rock* was playing on the small TV up in the corner above the bar. Paul took a long drink of his beer and set it down.

"We're getting out of here as soon as Devin and Lisa show up."

"Okee doke."

Leo scratched the back of his neck and gestured towards Kevin.

"You manage to get your hands on a season ticket?"

"Yeah, bought Brian's. Wasn't going to be much use for him in Boston."

Paul nodded.

"Nice. How much?"

"Three fifty."

"Not bad."

"Better than the eight-hundred I spent last year. Sold them to me at cost."

Leo and Paul started debating the highs and lows of Nicholas Cage's career, each sarcastic point punctuated with a genial laugh. Kevin checked his phone. Tracy Windy was still there.

ok...I am from Los Angeles which work are you doing there

Kevin sat back and tried to think of the most boring career choice possible. Something believable, but preferably giving hints of doing well enough to keep Tracy on the hook. He wished he had bought a beer. Too late now though. Lisa and Devin were on their way.

Here I am accountant. You?

Kevin thought the broken english added a nice touch. A nice little jab to show the perosn on the other end that he was fucking with them. It felt similar to seeing how close one could get their hand to a candle without getting burned. Lisa and Devin walked through the bar door, the old drunks raising their heads as they passed. Paul waved to get their attention, and then nudged Kevin to get him to stand up.

"Time to go."

Devin took Leo by the arm and Lisa grabbed on to Paul. Kevin was the odd man out. It was raining hard outside, the sky a darkening shade of gray. They put up their hoods and made their way across Burnside to the stadium, standing in wet lines before making their way through metal detectors into the interior. Most of the general seating area was already filled. They climbed their way upwards to close to the top. Kevin took careful note of the section they were in, 207, just in case he left for food or beverage. The rain was really coming down, big sheets pouring off parts of the roof covering the stands. The ladies went back down to get some food, leaving a scarf to cover their claimed seats on the long bench. The Timbers came out onto the field. People farther down started to sing. Leo stared at the roster handed out when they came inside, matching names to numbers. There were a lot of new faces. The ladies came back with popcorn. Leo and Paul went down and came back with beers. The crowd sang the national anthem and the game got underway. Kevin checked his phone once they were about fifteen minutes in.

really……I am student here doing my master degree please can you send me your pic

Shit. Kevin wasn't sure how to proceed. He really didn't want to send the random asshat on the other end a picture of himself. They'd probably just end up in some new fake profile. Hell though, two could play at that game. Kevin did a Google Image search for "handsome guy doing selfie" and through the results until he found one that he liked. It was a younger guy with brown eyes, probably early to mid-twenties. Longish tousled brown hair. A hint of five o'clock shadow. A round earring in each ear. From the bare shoulders and background it could be surmised that the guy was sitting shirtless on a couch, some kind of abstract painting hanging on a white wall behind his head. Perfect. Now he just needed to send it. Kevin tapped Leo with his elbow. Leo turned his head.

"What?"

"How do you save your screen?"

"Hit the front and top button at the same time."

"Thanks."

Leo glanced down at Kevin's phone. The handsome selfie gazed back at him.

"What the hell are you doing?"

"Some Nigerian scammer is messaging me, so I've just been fucking with him back."

Kevin showed Leo the supposed pictures of Tracy Windy and let him scroll through the messages so far. Leo just snorted, gave back the phone, and went back to watching the game.

"Tell her to send you some tit pics."

Kevin gave a smirk and went back to work. He took a screenshot and sent it. The moment he hit the send button he realized he had fucked it up. The sent picture was of his entire screen; time, battery life, even the search bar with "handsome guy doing selfie" written across it. Shit. The jig was up. The fun was probably over.

The crowd around him burst into an uproar. Timbers' goal! Timbers' goal! High fives all around. Kevin put his phone back into his coat pocket and went down the stairs to buy a beer. One sixteen ounce beer was ten dollars. Kevin bought two. You were allowed to have two at a time. He went back to his seat and drank both down, dropping the cups at his feet and kicking them underneath the bench. The Timbers scored again before the half. As the players filed off the field, the stands erupted into frenzied cheering that fell silent the moment the last green suited player disappeared from view. Kevin got back out his phone. Much to his surprise, Tracy Windy had left another message.

good and nice pic how old are you there

It was insane. How desperate were these people? Maybe it wasn't that, maybe it just didn't matter if he was lying. What difference did it make if he still fell for the scam?

29

really...are you single man there
Yes

That part wasn't a lie. Kevin had been single for nearly a year. Sure he had found a girl here and there for a good time, but nothing much beyond that. It wasn't that he wasn't trying, he just hadn't had much luck, that's all.

okay...do you searching for woman here
Here?

yes I am also single woman

Now they were making progress. This wasn't some kind of Nigerian prince scam. This was the old prey on a poor lonely sap scam. It made sense given the pictures. Kevin pulled them up and scrolled through them again. What poor sad son of a bitch wouldn't want some attention from an attractive woman?

No way.

what do you mean are you looking for serious relationship here

Maybe. I never thought about it before.
ok...how long are you been here searching for woman
Never searched for one before on here

okay...that mean I am a luck woman

:)

Jesus they laid it on thick. Kevin sent the emoticon to give himself time to think. How pathetic did someone have to be to fall for such horseshit? The players came back out and the second half got started. Devin and Leo were standing close together, their arms around each other's backs. Leo leaned over and gave Devin a peck on the cheek. Kevin looked away, embarrassed for watching.

do you wish know each other

Sure.

I am searching for mature man and looking for serious relationship

Kevin laughed quietly to himself. Sure, wasn't everybody.

Good. I only believe in serious relationships

yes...I wan relationship for my self

Better than asking for someone else.

Silence from Tracy Wind. She obviously didn't get the joke. Christ, what was he doing, telling jokes to a fucking scammer? The thought made Kevin a little uncomfortable. Best to get things moving along. He wanted to get to the ask.

Tell me more about myself. Oops. Yourself.

good....you sound good

What the hell was that supposed to mean?

Tell me more about yourself

okay...I will tell you about self...now Hello just a little more about me...well am mixed races, my mum is from cape/town where I went to school over thee the name of my school is Career College of Northern Nevada Address were is located 1987-A Corporate,Boulevard Nevada city Reno,and i relocated to Florida /Ponte Vedra over years now and my dad was a foreigner a US citizen though African/American, but late now,

What the fuck was all that gobbledy-gook? There obviously wasn't much training to be a scammer. Kevin Googled the supposed college. It actually existed, and even the address was correct, so apparently the person on the other end wasn't a complete moron. Still, though, it was all just so ridiculous.

Very cool. What do you study?

Architect

Kevin went back down the stairs and got himself two more beers for another twenty dollars. He pulled back out his phone when he got up to their seats.

tell me more about you and I will continue about my self I ve alot of story to share with you

Kevin drank down one of his beers. What would be the story of someone who would fall for this type of scam? What type of person would they be looking for?

I made some mistakes earlie on. Was married rite out of college, but she left me for a friend.

Kevin thought his misspellings were a nice touch. He looked back over her pictures again. There was one selfie where the camera was pointing down, her eyes covered by a yellow hat. She was wearing a black sports bra and black tights. Her long dark hair hung down over her tits. It looked like she was sucking in her stomach for the photo. There was a slight gap between her front teeth. Very sexy. Kevin wondered again who the woman was really.

ohh...that is very bad...now things we change

That be nice. Life better now

would lie continue to tell you about me is

Sure

I was in a 4years relationship,I am tracy windy t by name, 28 years old by my age and i am an Economist by my profession,I am competent economist by my profession and i have once worked in textile store, a collection of textiles design and sewing materials and i was lay off job in last year December 17th and hunt for job,

Kevin burst out laughing. He couldn't help it. Leo looked over, so Kevin showed him the latest message. Leo laughed too, gaining everyone else's attention. Kevin let each of them scroll through the messages. Paul and Lisa seemed to think it was all pretty funny. Devin was overall less interested. Tracy Windy had made a fatal mistake. Kevin was curious how she was going to get out of this one.

I thought you said you were an architect.

Silence on the other end. No response. Well, that was that. Kevin put his phone back in his pocket and went back to watching the game. The Timbers won five to one. A blowout. The crowd started singing victory songs before the game was even over. The masses moved back out onto the streets in a high mood, exuberant and cheering. Kevin and his friends walked back across Burnside to Tony's. They sat down in the same booth they had been sitting in before the game. More people came in. It was Friday. The Timbers had won. All was right in the world. Paul bought everybody a round. Kevin sat in the corner of the booth, Lisa crammed between him and Paul. Lisa grinned at Kevin.

"Anything more from your girlfriend?"

"Let me check. I think I scared her off."

Kevin pulled out his phone. He was wrong. Tracy Windy hadn't given up yet. She was persistent. Lisa leaned over to read over his shoulder, her breast sitting on his arm. Kevin didn't move his arm. Lisa didn't move her breast. She seemed not to notice. Kevin glanced at Paul, who was discussing something with Leo. Kevin didn't have any designs on Lisa. She was his good friend's fiancé. He wasn't that type of guy. Still though, it felt nice, the feeling of closeness.

yeah...that is my first degree now am doing my master degree tell me more about you

Lisa laughed.

"Yeah, because that's a normal move."

Kevin laughed too. Lisa took a sip of her drink.

"What are you going to say now?"

Leo piped up from the other side of the table.

"Tell her you used to fuck goats."

Kevin ignored Leo. He didn't want to get too outrageous. He wanted to see how far things would go.

I used to be into a lot of drugs, but cleaned myself up a few years back. Now only do pot occasionally

okay...what are you doing for living now and please are you real

Kevin read the message out loud. The whole table erupted into laughter. Even Devin gave a halfway grin. Leo chortled.

"Christ, it's like *Inception* or something."

Kevin sat for a moment, and then started typing.

Work as an accountant. Yes real. R u real?

Iam real becos alot of guys use to lair

Leo got up and bought another round for everybody. Kevin tried to decipher what Tracy was trying to say. He wasn't sure how to answer, and most of the suggestions weren't all that good. Lisa and Devin started talking about something else. The weight of Lisa's breast left his arm. Another message popped up. Tracy was getting impatient.

are you still there

Kevin looked through Tracy's photos again. She had a nice rack on her. He wondered what it would feel like to have her pressed up close, the weight of her breast on his arm. The photo of her and the kid caught his eye.

Yes. Looked at u photos. Is that yr kid?

yes I got only one kids what of you do you ve kids

Lisa leaned back over.

"Where we at with your girlfriend?"

Kevin read the last few messages out loud. Leo grinned.

"Tell her you're a chi-mo."

Devin punched Leo in the arm. Kevin gave him a dirty look.

231

"I'm not going to do that."

"Why the hell not?"

"I'm just not going to."

"It's not like you're going to be able to say anything that they're not going to reply to. Let me see your phone."

"What are you going to do?"

"Just trust me. I'll type something and let you look at it before hitting send."

"Why don't you just tell me?"

"Why don't you just trust me?"

The two glared at each for a moment. Leo laughed and got up to take a pee. Kevin went back to his phone. He was starting to get bored. Why the hell was he still pushing it along? Maybe Leo was right.

No kids. Got a donkey named Leslie.

It did no good.

ok...are you ready to listing with me

Sure.

good dear

Dear. Christ, had anyone ever called him dear?

I was born and raised up in USA but presently Los Angeles But am planing to move to state or relocate to any where as soon as i have meet my dream man or responsible honest, loyal caring man that i can spend all the rest of my life with and commit and dedicate all my life unto him,

Jesus. Tracy was really falling apart. It almost sounded a little desperate. How desperate and lonely would someone have to be? How nice would it be if things actually worked in such a way? How great if when you were feeling the lowest, some random woman just contacted you on Facebook? It would be a great story. The kind you'd love telling other people every chance you got. No, it's true, we met on Facebook by random. She was just messaging random people. Crazy right? It was time to put an end to it once and for all.

What about blowjobs?

Tracy Windy's profile picture stared up at him. He could see her big brown eyes staring up at him. He could see her lips with their soft pink lipstick around him.

yeah...I was working with one company before but now presently I want not working any more again

No. No. Oral sex.

what do you mean,

Kevin stared down at his phone. He was starting to run out of battery, and he needed to make sure he had enough to get a Lyft home. It was time to stop. It wasn't really all that funny anymore. His friends were getting ready to leave.

Never mind. Going to bed now.

alright dear, nice to meet you

They hit a few more bars after Tony's, then went to a pretty nice Japanese restaurant and had dinner. At about one in the morning Kevin caught a Lyft home. It cost twenty-five bucks. The smiling face of Tracy Windy filled his mind as he drifted off to sleep. She was just a fucking scammer. The scum of the Earth.

The concrete room had ten computers, all different makes and models. Some scavenged together from several different machines. The constant whirring of fans filled the background. All was lit by bright fluorescent lights that never turned off. A single small window sat high in one wall. Too high to look through. It was raining outside. It had been raining for the past two days straight. Seventeen year old Kabelo knew that the streets outside that weren't paved were probably a sea of mud by now. It would be bad for the people sleeping outside, the people with nowhere else to go.

The clock on Kabelo's computer said ten minutes until eight in the morning. The day shift would be coming in soon. The day shift had the better time, Europe and the Middle East. North

America used to be better, but some of the people who had been at it awhile said things were changing there. Kabelo believed it. He had hoped that the America was wearing down, but he had missed his chance. That was what it was, a game of wearing down. Die Kwenkawu had drilled the strategy into their heads. All you had to do was find somebody desperate enough to believe, and the rest would take care of itself. Find someone who was lonely. The more they posted, the lonelier they probably were. Draw them in. Make them feel special. Make them feel appreciated. When the time is right, tell them that you want to be with them, that you can't live without them. Tell them that you love them, that all you need is for them to send you some money for a plane ticket. That's all you need for the two of you to be together. It was harder than it sounded. Kabelo hadn't managed to get it to work yet. Soon though, hopefully soon.

The people at the computers were switching out. Phaswane waited impatiently for Kabelo to move. Kabelo knew that if he didn't move quickly enough then Phaswane would complain to Die Kwenkawu. Kabelo didn't want that to happen. He logged off of Tracy Windy's Facebook profile and got up. The older man pushed past him and sat down. Phaswane had been at for quite some time. He was good at it. That's why he got to work the day shift. That's why he got to fish in the Middle East, people so flush with oil money and a sense of male entitlement that they had no common sense. Phaswane always said that people with money were always the easier marks. Of course some random woman would message you, why the hell not? Money made people greedy. Money made people desperate. Money made people lonely.

Kabelo thought about the people stuck out in the rain again. He had once been one of those people. Not anymore, but possibly once again. Kabelo shivered. He was closing in on a month. Die Kwenkawu gave you a month to show you could make some money. If you didn't make any money, then you were no use to Die Kwenkawu. You had to prove yourself. If you proved yourself, Die Kwenkawu would be a little more forgiving when you hit a dry spell. You wouldn't necessarily get kicked out. His first week Kabelo had seen Die Kwenkawu beat the shit out of a young man named Mongane. Die Kwenkawu was a very hands on boss.

Kabelo left the computer room and went into the dormitory. It looked much the same as the computer room, only filled with cots instead of computers. A counter with a faucet and a row of plugged in hot plates with pots on them lined one wall. No fluorescent lights were lit, but two high windows on either side kept the room from getting dark. Two doors sat opposite the one to the computer room. One led to the bathroom, the other to Die Kwenkawu's office and the door to the outside world.

Kabelo took a pot from a hot plate and filled it with water. The pot was dirty, but not too bad. The cupboards below the counter were stuffed full of instant noodles, the cheapest available in Johannesburg. Kabelo cooked his noodles and ate them right out of the pot. His friend Karel came in and did the same. Karel looked tired. Kabelo tried to smile at his friend.

"Get any bites today?"

"Got one, an old man from Toronto."

"Where's that?"

"Canada I think. Got him to send me $200 to help me with my mother's surgery. What about you?"

"A few nibbles. I thought I was going to land one, but he went to bed before I could. Maybe I'll get him tomorrow."

Karel tried to smile, but his eyes gave him away.

"Maybe."

Kabelo felt worried, but he tried not to show it. Five more days. Karel knew it too. They had started the same day. Both finished eating. Karel sat down in a corner to read by the light from one of the windows. Kabelo stretched and made his way over to the cots to sleep. He was tired. Twelve hours was a long shift. The cot was still warm. The thin blanket stank like Phaswane. Kabelo wrapped an old t-shirt around his head to try and block out the light. The writing on the t-shirt said *Carolina Panthers Super Bowl XXXVIII Champion.* Tomorrow he would do better. Tomorrow he would get the lonely American to send him money. Maybe it would be for a plane ticket, or maybe an operation like Karel. Kabelo didn't want to go back outside.

They said Die Kwenkawu had once been just like all of them. They said that he had once been a street kid who had worked his way up via scams. Once he had been shit, now they said he lived in a big house and had a white girlfriend in Pretoria. Die Kwenkawu was an important man. People on the street respected Die Kwenkawu. Kabelo wanted to be just like his boss. His mother, if she had still been alive, would have called it stealing, but Die Kwenkawu said they were only taking a little. People in other countries had so much money, they weren't going to miss a little.

Kabelo tried to go to sleep. The face of Tracy Windy floated through his mind. He didn't know who the lady in the pictures actually was. It didn't matter. They were Tracy Windy now. Tracy Windy had everything. Tracy Windy had a college education. Tracy Windy had a car. Tracy Windy had a son who adored her. All Tracy Windy lacked was someone to love her. He'd get the money from the American tomorrow. Then he would be able to stay. She'd help him become just as successful as Phaswane. He'd save his money and buy a car, then maybe he'd get an education, and a job where he wouldn't have to scam people. Kabelo was going to be somebody. Tracy Windy would see to that. Her smiling white face with its big brown eyes filled his head until he fell asleep.

Sorry Bro

Paul sat on the bathmat, the details of the bathroom around him sharpened into hyper-clarity. The black and white hexagon tiles that made up the floor. A single long blonde hair in the corner where the black outnumbered the white. The map of the world shower curtain, orange shower stains slowly creeping north from the Antarctic. The sink on its pedestal, the bottom covered in dust. The mirror of the medicine cabinet flecked by toothpaste and god knows what else. The socket with its red and black circuit breaker buttons. The toilet paper roll hung in the improper underhanded fashion. The light reflecting off of the white porcelain of the toilet, a Jesus candle on top of the tank, a joke left behind at their housewarming party over a year ago. The seat was up. Lisa didn't like it when he left the seat up. She always joked that it was when he had started putting it down for her that she knew he was the man she was going to marry.

Paul was always doing little things like that for her. It was how he showed he loved her. He wasn't a man for grand gestures. He had never planned an elaborate Valentine's Day, sang her favorite song to her at a crowded karaoke bar, or left cutesy little love notes in her lunch. Such things weren't Paul. No, Paul was a man of foot rubs, putting spiders in glasses to take them safely outside, and cooking dinner and doing the dishes in the same night. Little favors that when added together built themselves into a crescendo of fondness and affection. Take this very night for instance. Paul's flight from San Francisco didn't get in until midnight. A lesser man might've wanted to see his wife at baggage claim. Not Paul. He came home quietly, careful not to wake his slumbering bride as he eased the key into the lock and prepared himself for the warmth of their marital bed.

Lisa was snoring softly in the bedroom. She always snored softly when she slept on her back. It was dark, but in his mind Paul could see her laying there, half covered by the quilt her mother had made them. Her eyes closed. Her lips slightly parted. Her long blonde hair spread out around her head like a halo. Paul could feel each inhale and exhale. The rush of air through her sinuses, down through the lovely length of her neck, lifting her chest upward. Paul could see himself standing over her. He could see his hands gripping her throat. He could feel her starting to struggle. He could feel himself starting to scream.

Bile built at the back of Paul's throat. He banished the dark dream back into the unlit recesses of his mind. It wasn't the first to bubble to the surface since he had fallen to the bathroom floor. Punching her again and again. Him on top of her, fucking away as she cried. A single shot from a pistol that didn't exist. They crowded their way forward, unsettling his stomach and twisting his psyche until tears rolled down his cheeks, all that was good in him begging for it all to stop.

He had to pee. He hadn't done it yet. It seemed insane that such a thing could still demand such attention, but the basic needs of the body would always outdo the whirling maelstrom of the mind no matter how chaotic. He couldn't do it. He couldn't face it again. He didn't want to look. He didn't want to see. The pressure in his bladder swelled to greater proportions, locked in a battle it knew it was going to win. Paul rose and stood by the toilet. He stared at the picture of narwhals on the wall, refusing to let his eyes waver. It wasn't real. It was a mistake. A bad joke. Anything but the truth.

Paul looked. He couldn't help himself. It was instinct. A habit born of thousands of repetitive actions. The words were still there. The cursed words arching their way around the bottom of the toilet seat, letters in cherry red lipstick, the shade she had worn on their second anniversary two months before. It had been a wonderful night. Such a wonderful evening. They had gone to the City Grill in its tower. Her in a tight dress that left little to the imagination and he in the suit he almost never wore. They had come home floating on a sea of champagne. They had made love on the floor of the living room, neither able to wait the last twenty feet to the bed.

With a shiver he was done. The tears became a storm. A murderous cacophony of emotion, though still he didn't make a sound, not wanting to wake her, wanting to hold on to the last threads as long as possible. He collapsed down again, his back against the towels hanging on the wall, the bright red letters blazing in front of him, strobing in time with the wild beat of his heart.

Sorry bro, she didn't tell me she was married.

Previously Published Works

Evidence
First published in *Permafrost Magazine*, Summer 2017

Dan The Man
First published in *Permafrost Magazine*, Winter 2018

When Is It Due
First published in *Linden Avenue*, Issue 75, August 2018

Gutterball
First published in *Santa Clara Review*, Winter 2019

Simple Syrup
First published in *Cirque Journal*, December 2019

Margarita Monday
First published in *Pilgrimage Magazine*, Volume 43, Issue 1, Summer 2020

Dates Written

Glimpses of Morning	May 2013
Slap Fight	November 2013
Lost Dog	January 2014
Margarita Monday	July 2013
Peaches	September 2015
The Champion	June 2015
A View Of Paradise	March 2013
Dan The Man	May 2016
Probably Crazy	March 2014
Gobshite	September 2015
Protest	February 2017
When Is It Due	March 2016
Gutterball	June 2016
Dancer	January 2014
How Was Montana	November 2015
Bogey At Ten O'Clock	March 2013
Vanity	July 2016
Evidence	January 2016
Bad Start	January 2017
Respite	March 2013
A Good Old Fashioned Ash Whooping	July 2017
Simple Syrup	May 2017
Insert Title Here	November 2017
Scammer	March 2017
Sorry Bro	May 2018

Also Written By The Author

The Uncanny Valley

We all know a Paul. A person who seems to see stuff that isn't there. The type the polite call quirky and the blunt call nuts. Conspiracies? He's got a few. He's got his finger on how the world really works. He knows what kind of shit is coming down the pipe. Flee across the West Texas desert to Mexico? Makes sense to him. Feel like you're being watched? You bet your ass someone is watching. Best turn off your cellphone. Troubles? Of course, that's just part of life. Doubts? No time for doubts. Shit is getting real. Get in, buckle up, crack open a beer. The only real question is, how far down the rabbit hole are you willing to follow?

An Unsated Thirst

They say that an author's first stories are their most raw. Here is a collection of S.W. Campbell's first short stories and writings. Combining both published and unpublished works, An Unsated Thirst explores victory and defeat, triumph and shame, and an unflinching view of our naked selves. How one views such stories is dependent upon the mood of the reader. Whether we are at our highs or at our lows. However, it is hard for any of us to claim that such stories are ones that we cannot identify with. Contained within these pages are parts of our lives which we try to forget, though they are an important part of what makes us whole. Such stories should be embraced, accepted within ourselves so we can better accept them with others.

Papaya

When a devastating hurricane hits the CAribbean island of Domenique, its inhabitants are forced into a singular struggle to survive and rebuild. Isolated in their midst is Ted, a Peace Corps volunteer who fled the ashes of his former life only to find himself labeled an outsider. Infatuated by the enigmatic wife of his only friend, Ted thrusts himself into a world beyond his comprehension. As obsession turns to desperation, tensions grow and Ted is forced to decide exactly how far he will go to rebuild amidst the muddy ruins.

Professor Errare Presents…45 Jerks And Counting

The President of the United States of America. It has to be one of the hardest jobs in the world. You're under never ending pressure, you get blamed for everything, people hate your guts no matter what you do, and to top it all off, it ages you faster than meth. What kind of person would want a job like that? I'll tell you who, a jerk. The U.S. of A. has had 45 presidents so far in its history, and all have had one thing in common. They've all been jerks. This satirical book is not here to tell you about the great things that each president did. No, it's here to make you question how these people ever got to be leaders, and more importantly, what the hell is wrong with us for electing them. Enjoy.

Professor Errare Presents...40 American Jackasses Worth Knowing

There is probably no greater American tradition than that of being a jackass. Where else in the world is a jackass truly free to reach their full potential of jackassery? Throughout our country's history men and women have risen to the braying call of infamy, willing to put it all on the line to prove.....well..... we're really not all that sure. This satirical book is here to tell you about some of the greatest of these All-American jackasses, with a few people who had to deal with everybody around them being a jackass thrown in for good measure. Read it, enjoy it, and perhaps even be inspired to find out just how much of a jackass you yourself can be.

Professor Errare Presents...And Then What Happened

What happened to Lewis and Clark after their famous cross-country expedition? How did an imaginary cult help cause the Black Death? What happened to Al Capone after he got sent to prison? What's this I hear about Napoleon's dick? There are certain moments in history that pretty much everybody knows about, even that idiot who lives next door to you. This book isn't about those moments. No, this book is about the crazy parts leading up to or following those events that have been mostly left out of the history books. If you're tired of the general whitewashing of history into some kind of epic heroic journey, well then this is the perfect book for you.

Professor Errare Presents…Random History

Have you ever been beaten up by a bunch of young hoodlums for wearing a straw hat? Why in the hell are so many manicure shops owned by Vietnamese? Why is that old timey doctor drinking your urine? How in the heck did we let the savior of the world die in a crappy apartment in a suburb in Moscow? Do all of these questions sound random as all get out? Good, because this is a book on the random history. In these pages are the random tidbits left out of the history books for being too scandalous, too risque, and too unbelievably weird. So what are you waiting for? Open it up. Start reading. It's about damn time you started learning worth knowing.

Professor Errare Presents…Stuff You Should Know

So you think you know a little bit about history. You've got this all pretty figured out. All the dots connect in a nice neat little line. Well guess what bucko, if that's your attitude than you probably know diddly squat. Do you know about how hookworms led to common stereotypes? What about the weird cult that makes silverware? Why so many art students feel like it's okay to be crazy dicks? Do you know about Hilter's farts? If you're answer is no, then this is the book for you. Generally most of us having a basic understanding of history centered around memorized dates. However, as they say, the devil's in the details. Maybe it's time you sat down and learned some stuff you should know.

More information can be found at:

www.shawnwcampbell.com

About The Author

S.W. Campbell was born in Eastern Oregon in 1983 after a harrowing drive through a fog. He currently resides in Portland, Oregon where he works as an economist and lives with a lovely house plant named Morton. He has had several short stories published in various literary reviews, some of which appear in this work, and has also self-published several books. His work can be found at www.shawnwcampbell.com.

www.ingramcontent.com/pod-product-compliance
Lightning Source LLC
Chambersburg PA
CBHW071557110726
47908CB00007B/2136